the APPLE doesn't FALL FAR

Mary Ellen Bramwell

Black Rose Writing | Texas

First printing

ISBN: 978-1-68433-805-4
PUBLISHED BY BLACK ROSE WRITING
www.blackrosewriting.com

Printed in the United States of America
Suggested Retail Price (SRP) $18.95

The Apple Doesn't Fall Far is printed in Adobe Caslon

*As a planet-friendly publisher, Black Rose Writing does its best to eliminate unnecessary waste to reduce paper usage and energy costs, while never compromising the reading experience. As a result, the final word count vs. page count may not meet common expectations.

To Janyce Maxfield Harrison

My cheerleader from the other side

the
APPLE
doesn't
FALL FAR

BROKEN

The window stood slightly ajar. Brea preferred the cool night air for sleep. But sleep would not come, not tonight.

Troubled, she threw off her covers then pulled them back up. She turned on her right side then switched to the left. Thrashing about then finally lying still, Brea was unsure why she couldn't settle. She strained her ears to pick out the distant night sounds—a cat meowing, hissing, followed by the unmistakable yowls of a cat fight; a dog barking; the occasional whine of a passing car, one clearly the neighbor's that needed a new engine, its knocking and pinging familiar to her. The noises were not unusual, but sleep still eluded her.

Her breathing grew ragged, quickening in nervousness, slowed only by conscious effort. *What is wrong with me? I haven't had a night like this in years, not since … not since the night Paul died.* But that was over a dozen years ago. She'd made peace with that already. Still, she struggled to breathe normally, fighting the urge to gasp for air.

Like a thief approaching in the night, the breeze in her room shifted. Her curtains at first waved a gentle hello then a fierce warning before letting loose a frantic modern dance in her bedroom, their shadows snaking back and forth across her bedsheets. Brea shivered and forced herself to take a deep, steadying breath.

It will stop, surely it will stop. But the wind grew stronger as her breathing grew weaker. Climbing out of bed, she darted to the open window. Curtains whipped at her face and arms as she struggled to force the window closed. She could see the trees outside, angry, fighting the encroaching storm.

Flash! Crack! The lightning streaked across the sky in front of her, throwing her backward in fright, the curtains twisting around her. She screamed, but a sickening roar of thunder swallowed the sound. Another flash lit the night, illuminating her bedroom, immediately coupled with deep-throated thunder and a wrenching, eerie sound like a choked-off earthen sob.

Shaking, she collapsed to the carpet, unable to rise. Rain dampened the swaying curtains, falling in cold droplets onto her bare toes.

Determined, she gritted her teeth and said aloud, "I am not that same naïve young thing. I am strong." Standing, she strode to the window and yanked it closed. The curtains dropped still against her back and arms, the wet patches left by the rain sticking to her bare skin. She stood motionless, gradually regaining control of her breathing when another flash startled her. In its split-second light, she saw the apple tree in the middle of her backyard—the one she'd planted with Noah to always remind them of their husband and father, the one that for a decade had produced an abundance of delicious apples. But in that one illuminating moment, she'd seen, not the tree she was used to, but a frightening image with limbs askew.

She gasped. Not that apple tree, Paul's apple tree! She watched for further flashes but none came. Out in the darkness, her tree had cried out in pain. She'd heard it. Its voice diverged sharply from the thunder, a low, guttural, earthly sound like no other.

Shivering, Brea climbed back into bed, pulling the covers up around her shoulders, the continuing storm making sleep elusive. Finally, as the storm subsided in the early morning hours, Brea's frayed nerves relaxed, and she fell into a fitful sleep, dreaming of broken promises.

TIME WILL TELL

Brea's alarm jerked her awake at seven. Immediately she felt despair in the pit of her stomach. Throwing on yesterday's clothes, she raced downstairs and out the back door. As she feared, the storm had been ruthless. Several once-healthy limbs from her precious apple tree lay twisted and scattered on the ground, severed from the main trunk with a large, blackened gash.

She collapsed onto the wet ground, waiting for the sobs to come. But they didn't. She was simply numb.

To the left and the right of Paul's tree stood two other apple trees, planted later to aid in pollination. Neither, it appeared, was damaged other than a few spare twigs strewn about their roots.

Noah was stirring in the kitchen behind her. His school started soon, and she needed to see him off. But the disaster in front of her was more compelling. She got up and walked around the tree, running her hands over its wounded trunk. Leaves were plentiful in early May, but it hadn't started to blossom yet. Now, who knew if it ever would again.

Her husband, Paul, had died young—too young, when Noah was only six months old. It was well over a year after his death when she finally went a day without thinking about him. The realization that twenty-four hours had passed without memories washing over her had been comforting yet frightening. It meant she could move on. She could have a life and function. She could smile without also shedding a tear.

It also meant she *was* moving on, that the tears wouldn't come so readily, that she was forgetting. With that fresh fear, she had scooped up Noah, a toddler at the time, and taken him out to the apple tree in the backyard. Under the afternoon sun of late summer, she had spread a blanket on the ground next to the tree she and Noah planted together on his first birthday.

They often lounged in that very spot, but this day was different. Brea began to tell Noah, not quite two, stories about his daddy. Noah knew who the pictures scattered around the house were, hugging and kissing them on a regular basis. But he didn't know who his daddy was, what he was like, what he cared about. His father was a two-dimensional image in a frame and nothing more.

Before the memories faded, Brea shared them with Noah. Then at night while he slept, she typed frantically on her laptop, writing everything she could remember—the highs and the lows.

Paul had died in the spring—typically a time of rebirth not death. But so much of life is not as it appears.

. . .

"Mom? What are you doing?" Noah's voice shook her memories loose. "Mom? I'm going to be late for school."

Brea quickly moved to the front of the tree to block its damage from view—as if such a thing were remotely possible. But she needn't have bothered. It appeared Noah had called to her without seeing what had captured her attention.

After dropping Noah off at the Summerhill Middle School, she turned toward home. Noah was a sweet child, thirteen and thriving in eighth grade— or at least so she thought and hoped. His grades were generally good, but he'd become quieter and more withdrawn lately. Wondering if there was something under the surface was a concern she rarely allowed herself to consider. She prayed this had more to do with him becoming a teenager than anything else.

Instead of turning down her street, she drove past it, making a beeline for the nearby apple orchard. It took a few minutes of wandering around to find the owner, Mr. Charles, in his maintenance shed. He moved a little slower than he had a dozen years before when he'd given her the apple tree along with planting instructions. She'd gone back to him the next year once she'd finished writing about Paul's life. He recommended two more apple trees then refused payment, calling them a birthday present for her fatherless two-year-old.

Once her trees matured, she'd had no need to purchase apples from his orchard, but she did anyway, combining them with her own to make and preserve applesauce and apple pie filling. He would pretend to have forgotten the actual price for his apples, and Brea humored him while still handing him double the posted amount.

"Mr. Charles?"

He looked up from his workbench. "Well, hello, Brea. How's Noah?"

"He's fine, I think." He raised an eyebrow expecting more information, but she had a different focus today. "Mr. Charles. It's my tree, the first one."

He stroked his beard, peering at her. "What's wrong? It still should be bearing a strong harvest, and it's not even time for it to bloom yet."

Brea started to speak, but her voice caught in her throat. The tears she'd expected that morning came flooding out in place of words.

Mr. Charles got up and gently put a hand on her shoulder. "Was it the storm?"

She nodded. "Paul's tree. It … it's damaged. Lightning."

"How bad?"

"I don't know," she said, shaking her head. "It's black and burned, but not all of it."

"Well, let me go have a look see." He grabbed an old baseball cap and followed her out the shed door. "I'll grab my truck and meet you at your place."

. . .

Brea watched from the back porch as Mr. Charles pruned and trimmed like a barber taking a little off the sides. He examined it from all angles, paying careful attention to the new, brutal gash. When finished, he hauled the broken limbs to the back of his truck.

Only when the backyard was free of storm debris did he approach Brea. He was slowly stroking his beard.

"Can it be salvaged? Will it bear fruit again?"

"Time will tell. I'm sorry I can't say more. Time will tell."

"When will I know?"

"Watch for it to bloom. If it produces blossoms in a few weeks, it will be fine. If not … well, if not, it was a wonderful tree."

THE APPLE OF MY EYE

Brea was working in her home office when Noah walked in from school. He liked having his mom drive him to school in the mornings. It was quicker than the bus and therefore allowed him a little more shut-eye. But in the afternoons, he was content to arrive whenever the school bus happened to expel him.

"Hi, Noah. How was your day?" She stood in the doorway of her office watching him shed his backpack and shoes by the front door.

"Fine."

"Do you have a lot of homework?"

"No."

There had been a time not long ago when his answers not only had more than one syllable, they had a gush of words. Brea followed her son into the kitchen. "Would you like something to eat? I could make you nachos or you could have an apple."

Noah's head came up suddenly at her words. "An apple?"

"Yes. Mr. Charles had some in cold storage. They're nice and crisp." She reached up to ruffle his hair like she'd done since he was little, but he bristled slightly, and she pulled back just in time. "You're the apple of my eye, Noah. You'll never be too old for that."

He nodded and a slight smile escaped his lips. It was an expression of love Paul had used for both of them. And now its use expressed their love for each other along with a connection to Paul. Automatically Noah's head turned toward the backyard.

Brea let out a sigh. "Noah, will you come with me a minute, please?"

When he looked up expectantly, she opened the back door and led him outside. "Did you hear that storm last night?"

"Hard not to."

"The tree got hit with lightning. I guess the good news is it didn't go up in flames."

They stood together at the base of the tree. It had grown considerably in the years since they'd planted it, and the remaining limbs arched protectively over their heads.

"Mr. Charles cleaned it up today, but he doesn't know if it will produce apples again. He said, 'Time will tell.'"

Noah quickly glanced over the black wound, furtively brushing it with his fingers. Putting his hands in his pockets, he shrugged, spun and headed back inside. Brea had expected more of a reaction, but you never could tell. She didn't notice Noah biting his lip as he stepped back into the house.

Brea worked as a freelance programmer, starting shortly after Paul passed away. He'd left her financially well enough off that she could work when she wanted and not when she didn't, which meant she usually worked Monday through Friday from the time she dropped off Noah to when he came in the door at the end of his school day. But lately, he would head up to his room after grabbing a snack. To keep from worrying, she often returned to her office and logged another hour or two of work before dinner.

Watching Noah duck back inside, she knew it would be another one of his retreat-to-the-bedroom days. Without thinking, she headed to Martha's house next door for advice. Martha was her friend, sage, and confidant, and had been since Brea moved in, pregnant with Noah.

Brea knocked then entered without waiting for a response, as had been her habit for years. "Hello? Are you home?"

"Yes, Bree. I'm in the living room."

Brea abruptly halted. Her mother was the only one who had taken to calling her Bree lately, and it was her mother's voice she heard.

Of course it wasn't Martha's voice. It couldn't be. Martha had passed away six months ago at the age of 99. Brea's parents, Earl and Lizzie Roberts, finally retired, bought the place to be closer. But Brea's automatic reaction when she needed someone was still to head to Martha's, expecting to take a seat at her kitchen table and talk things out over tea and cookies or juice and muffins. It had taken her months to break the habit. And now the turmoil of the storm had set her back, reflex taking over in the moment of crisis.

Brea loved her mother. It was nice that she was here, and at least Martha was finally reunited with her husband after being a widow for twenty-four years. It was that thought alone that made her passing bearable for Brea.

Taking a deep breath, she stepped through the archway into the living room. "Hi, Mom. How's it going?"

"Great, sweetie." Lizzie stood to embrace her daughter, and Earl sitting nearby nodded to her. "Your dad and I were going over the plans for the backyard. Do you want to see?"

She didn't. She wasn't ready for Martha's yard to exist only in her memory. It was too much change.

"Bree, are you okay?"

"Umm … yeah, I'm okay." As grandparents, they saw Noah through rose-colored glasses. That was a good thing, for the most part. Dare she say something that could potentially alter that relationship?

"Then what's up? You're always welcome to walk right in, but … you don't usually do that," Earl said.

"I know, Dad. Sorry about that. Umm … I was just wondering about Noah. He's not talking to me much these days. I don't know what he's thinking or how he spends his time … or if he's hiding things from me. Should I be worried?"

Lizzie patted Brea's arm. "Certainly keep an eye on things, but that sounds pretty normal for a teenager. They need their space while they explore their independence." Earl nodded his agreement.

She should feel better, but she didn't. How could they be missing it?

"Okay, thanks. I guess it's not a big deal. I better get back to him." She spoke rapidly, her thoughts muddled, before making a hasty retreat.

Paul had hidden things.

She hadn't known his secrets until after he died. In fact, his secrets led to his death. She leaned against the porch railing of her parents' home trying to catch her breath, fighting the sense of rising bile in her stomach.

She retraced her steps to her backyard where the damaged apple tree taunted her. Would it produce more apples, or was its run now over? Once again, she ran her hand over the rough wood where the severed limb had been only a short time before. She couldn't suppress the dark thoughts any longer.

Was Noah like his dad? How far did that particular apple fall from the tree?

. . .

Paul was a good man. Brea knew that, without a doubt. He made mistakes along the way and had thrown in with the wrong people. But when he woke up to what was going on, he worked hard to fix it. His "friends" didn't take kindly to his change of heart, and it cost him his life. However, Brea knew that he died an honorable man. She had made peace with all that Paul had done and hadn't done. In the end, he put his love for her and Noah above all else.

But that didn't change the fact that his secretive behavior created a problem so big that he wasn't able to successfully back out of it. Noah knew about his father, and yet, did he really understand about his father?

Surely Noah was entitled to his secrets. She had been a teenager once too. And she didn't know a teenager alive who shared everything with his parents. She just didn't want Noah to end up in dangerous territory—especially territory he didn't know how to retreat from. She was uneasy with the rift between them, a rift with an unknown source.

"Hey, Noah?" Brea tapped lightly on her son's door. No response. "Noah?"

She was surprised when he abruptly opened his door but more surprised to see his backpack slung over his shoulder.

"I'm off to my friend's house."

Taken aback, Brea said, "What friend? Did you–"

"Yes, I asked you and I told you. I'll be back later."

He quickly maneuvered around her, but as he did so, a notebook fell out of his open backpack. Brea bent to pick it up. It had a dark-blue cover with no indication which school subject it might be for. "Noah, is this your notebook?"

Noah spun around, his eyes narrowed. "What are you doing with that?" He snatched it out of her hands.

"You dropped it. I didn't …"

He didn't wait to find out what she didn't do. He barreled down the stairs. By the time Brea made it down after him, all she caught of Noah was a faint glimpse of him out the window. He was riding off on his bike, the sun reflecting off his hair—wavy, auburn hair, just like his father's.

MARTHA'S BOX

Had Noah told her earlier he was going to a friend's, like he said? Brea couldn't be sure. Confused by these thoughts, she retreated to her office. There was still time before making dinner to get some work done. Only she couldn't focus.

At a loss, Brea made her way to her front porch and sat down on the steps. She felt the day fading, but the May sun irritatingly insisted on stretching it out before her. The sun warmed her when she wanted to feel cold. It illuminated the flowers blooming in her neat garden bed, their reds, whites, and purples threatening to put a smile on her face. She firmly fixed a frown on it instead.

She watched the workers from next door pack up their van with tools and empty coolers. When they pulled out, she wandered over to her parents' new home.

This time she knocked and waited to be let in. Feeling bad for her earlier abrupt departure, she embraced her dad when he let her in. "Hey, sorry to be in such a hurry before. How is the remodel going?"

"Great. Take a look around. We'll be in the kitchen. Your mom is trying to decide if she wants to change her countertop choice. She has two more days before it will be too late to change." He rolled his eyes.

"Which means she'll decide in two days."

"Exactly! It's like you know her or something." Earl chuckled.

"Yes, Lizzie Roberts is famous for being decisive—eventually." Brea smiled despite herself. "I'll meet you in the kitchen in a few minutes. I haven't seen your bedroom with the furniture in it yet."

"Okay. Help yourself to the tour."

Even though her parents bought the home six months ago, they had only recently moved in. Brea had offered to let them stay at her place, but they were still wrapping up the sale of their home and closing their business. Which meant they had been flying in and out, popping in for a night or two every couple weeks. And the time they had spent in town was mostly taken up with meetings with contractors to oversee the remodeling efforts.

Brea wandered into her parents' new master suite. The home had been built in a different era when having more bedrooms outweighed their size. So, they had taken two of those smaller bedrooms and a nearby bathroom and completely redone them into a beautiful master bedroom and luxury bathroom. Space from a mudroom next to it was now their walk-in closet. The transformation was stunning. With new furniture arriving a week ago, her parents had finally settled in.

She followed the sound of voices to the kitchen. It was in a state of disarray. Old cupboards and appliances had been removed and the plumbing and wiring were being replaced. Her parents sat on folding chairs poring over drawings on a card table amid the construction debris.

Martha's kitchen had been cozy, not because it was small but because it was comfortable. It was actually reasonably large with room for a generous table in a sunlit corner. Lizzie loved the space yet was making it her own, as was her right, Brea reminded herself.

But it was wrong. It was all wrong. While construction had been taking place on the new master suite, the workers largely left the kitchen alone. Brea could still walk in and be flooded by pleasant memories of Martha and all the time they'd spent together here, all the advice, the laughter, the love. But as the old kitchen was dismantled, her memories of Martha threatened to disappear as well. It felt like losing those wisps of Paul all over again.

She shook off the memories and smiled at her parents. It *was* wonderful to have them here all the time now. They had always been a huge blessing to her and Noah, and their close proximity would only increase that. Even though she knew it was Martha's time to go and her parents weren't trying to replace Martha, it was easy to forget that.

Lizzie lifted her gaze and acknowledged her daughter with a smile. "Do you want to see the latest plans? I've got some countertop samples you can weigh in on."

Brea chuckled softly. "In a minute."

She had one more room to visit first. Martha's bedroom, formerly the largest, was now the spare bedroom. It was essentially untouched and would remain so. Without saying it, her parents left it for her—a retreat, a reminder, whatever she needed it to be.

Brea entered it almost reverently, running her hand down the wall until she found the switch. Light flooded the room, and for a moment she saw it as it once was. Her parents had installed new carpet, but it was the same dusty brown color it had always been. And the painters had added a fresh coat of paint to the walls in the same pale yellow that Martha favored. Only the closet was left to repaint.

The room was empty of actual furniture, but Brea could see all the furnishings in her mind's eye. A double bed materialized in front of her, the headboard against the far wall with matching nightstands on either side. A wedding ring quilt neatly covered the bed, topped with an assortment of colorful pillows.

The double bed faded from her view and was replaced with the hospital bed that had been installed the last two months of Martha's life. Hospice had become the stable influence as Martha's children took turns staying with her in the house. Brea and Noah had been regular visitors, sometimes coming together but just as often separately.

Martha had been lucid up to the end. They would talk together until Martha's strength waned, but she hated for Brea to leave. So, Brea would often stay until Martha's eyes closed, leaving only once she knew Martha was merely sleeping, the soft sound of her breathing comforting.

Noah would come home from his solo visits in any number of moods—somber, laughing, thoughtful, or cheerful. Brea never asked what they talked about. Occasionally he told her anyway, recounting stories Martha told him about her childhood or antics from her children's lives. Brea didn't worry then about things he wasn't sharing with her because if they were being shared with Martha, they were nothing to fear.

Brea ran her hands over the smooth walls then moved toward the hospital bed that wasn't there anymore. She could picture herself standing at the foot of that bed six months ago. Martha's children had one by one been in to say goodbye. They had summoned Brea and Noah one last time.

With tears streaming down Brea's face, she and Noah had said their final goodbyes. Standing on either side of her, they each cradled one of her hands, kissed it, and then they kissed her cheeks, Brea's tears falling to roll down Martha's cheeks instead of her own. Martha's voice was weak, but the words, "I love you. Take care of each other," were strong in their ears. A feeling of joy permeated the room, overwhelming the sorrow. She was going home.

. . .

Brea wiped her eyes, and the room's empty interior reemerged. Curtains were the last remaining feature in the room. Without realizing what she was doing, she reached for the delicate drapery bringing it to her nose, but like everything else in the room, it was now devoid of the familiar smell of Martha's house—a combination of freshly-baked cookies and almond-scented lotion. Instead, her nose registered freshly laundered curtains, newly painted walls, and the unmistakable smell of brand-new carpet. Her parents had left the room intact for her, and yet it would never be the same.

Martha had a walk-in closet in her bedroom, even if by today's standards it would be considered more of a reach-in closet. Brea carefully opened its door, as if a bowling ball might fall on her head. It was empty like everything else.

The closet door stuck slightly on the newly-laid carpet that extended into the closet, bringing its scent along with it. The bare bulb inside was activated by a pull cord. The electrician planned on updating the wiring, connecting it to a switch, but it was low on the priority list.

Brea pulled the string. The light turned on while the string sprung back from her pull, popping up and lodging in a tangle on an upper closet shelf. She reached up, but it was out of her grasp.

Without disturbing her parents, she located a small step ladder in a hall cupboard. Dragging it back into the bedroom, she set it up in the small closet. As she climbed the few steps, she moved farther away from the new carpet and closer to the not-yet-repainted closet walls and shelves. A hint of Martha's fragrant lotion tickled her nose.

Smiling, she reached out to untangle and free the cord, the shelf underneath it dusty with grime. A shadow caught her attention. This shelf had been neglected. It was not empty, the remaining items visible from her position but not from below.

The first thing Brea touched was a sachet, like a small potpourri bag. It was meant to freshen the smell in the closet. Brea brought its dusty surface to her nose. The intended scents had long faded, and the dust made her sneeze.

Dropping it to the floor, Brea reached back to see what else she could find. Her fingers touched another dusty item. Pulling it out, she discovered an old collapsible umbrella. It appeared to have once been white and green but was now gray and greenish-gray. Sticky with grime, she dropped it to the carpet below her as well.

One last item rested on the shelf. As she touched it, her fingers felt the smooth surface of a box. It was oddly devoid of dust.

She tried to pick it up, but the sticky grime of the shelf held it firm. Reaching out with both hands, she yanked, and the box came free, almost causing her to lose her balance. Holding the box close, she descended the step ladder.

Sitting cross-legged on the bedroom floor, she examined the box in front of her. It was square, of a size that could hold a pair of child's shoes. Clearly belonging to a different era, it was covered with doilies and angels. But the old-fashioned decorations were not what caught her eye. In the middle of the lid, in Martha's familiar handwriting she read:

For Brea and Noah. Open together.

GEORGE HARRISON

With a hasty call to her parents of, "I'm heading back home. I'll have to check out those countertops later, Mom. Love you," she was out the door. She didn't even wait for their reply. She would have to make a conscious effort not to leave so abruptly again Brea thought, after realizing she'd done it twice in one day. And they hadn't actually lived next door that long.

She placed the box on her kitchen table, setting it down as if it would break, even though that was clearly not the case. What to do? She didn't know when Noah would be home. When he went to friends' houses, he often stayed through dinner. She could call him to come home, but that might come off as smothering, alienating him even more than he already was. She could text him and ask if he was coming home for dinner.

The last thing she wanted to do was irritate Noah unnecessarily. It seemed like she was doing plenty of that already. She figured he wouldn't be upset by Martha's box, but she didn't want him to be in a foul mood before she could even show the box to him.

Brea was not an uncertain person. Being a single mom for years had rooted any of that out of her—or so she'd thought. But this was new territory. Noah was blazing new territory for both of them. She was concerned about him, despite what her parents had said. But what exactly were the battles she needed to fight?

Obviously, this was not one of them. It wasn't even a battle. It was simply impatience on her part. She could wait.

Completely forgetting about preparing any kind of dinner, Brea left the box where she'd laid it. She retreated to the living room, picking up a book on the way. While waiting for Noah to return, Brea read twenty pages of her book, all without being able to recall a single word.

Assuming Noah would not make it home for dinner, although she wasn't even aware of the time, she picked up her phone. "Amy? Hey, I know it's last minute, but would you like to grab dinner?"

"Hey, girl. Man, I wish I could. Spencer is coming down with a cold, so I can't imagine leaving the twins with him. And Lia is such a mama's girl, that, well, you know. It's almost her bedtime anyway."

"No problem. I figured it was a long shot." Amy's twins were eight now, and little Lia was four. When Brea wasn't thinking, she forgot her friend had young children to consider.

"But we could try lunch tomorrow? Are you game? I'll have Lia with me, but D and D will be in school."

Amy and Spencer had long embraced their nerdiness. Playing dungeons and dragons had been how they'd first met. Not surprisingly, naming their twins Davis and Dani was one of their self-proclaimed more brilliant moves.

"Sure. Lunch sounds great." After deciding on when and where, Brea hung up. She had wandered into the kitchen while talking. Martha's box still sat on the kitchen table, its sight piquing her curiosity.

The sound of the door in from the garage startled her. Noah burst into the kitchen a moment later. "Hi, Mom."

"Hi, Noah." Her voice was distracted.

"Are you okay?" The warmth that had been missing earlier was back.

"Umm. Yeah, I am."

Noah peered behind her. "Dinner? Are we skipping it tonight?" It wasn't accusatory but rather playful.

"No, I didn't know if … if you were coming back for it."

"Sorry about that. I guess I was just having a bad day."

Brea raised his eyebrows at him, but he didn't elaborate. Should she push or not? She tried to find a middle ground. "Anything I can help with?"

He stiffened slightly, but then relaxed. "No."

"Well, let me throw some dinner together. I've got chicken in the fridge that will cook up fast."

"Hey, what's this?" He was pointing to the box on the table. "I remember seeing that at Mimi's house." Mimi is the name he'd called Martha since he was two.

"You did?"

"Yeah, a little before she went on hospice, when she could still get around the house on her own. It was on her kitchen counter, so I asked her about it."

"What did she say?"

"That it was an old treasure box she'd had for a long time." He shrugged. "You know, it was strange. Usually, something like that would be an excuse to launch into a story, but she didn't say anything else. I think she started feeding me cookies instead."

"Well, that part's not unusual." They both chuckled.

Noah picked up the box. He opened his mouth to say something else then paused. He'd seen what was written on top. Sinking into a kitchen chair, he grew quiet. Slowly he traced Martha's writing with his finger.

Brea sat down in a chair next to him, all thoughts of dinner forgotten. Noah lifted his head and their eyes met. Instead of speaking, they nodded to each other.

Together, with unspoken agreement, they lifted the lid. The smell of Martha hit them, bringing with it a flood of memories. They stared at each other, neither peeking into the box yet. "Ready?" Noah's voice came out as a whisper.

The box was full of envelopes. And on top was a folded piece of stationary. Noah looked expectantly at his mom. Brea carefully picked it up.

Dear Brea and Noah,

I love you both. You know that. If I haven't made that clear by now, something is terribly wrong. But that's not the purpose of this particular gift. This gift is one that will take time to discover, so you'd better get started.

I need to give you a few instructions. As you can see, the box is full of envelopes. Each envelope is numbered and labelled. Each is to be opened in order and by the recipient listed on the outside. Follow the instructions inside. (Don't ask me why, just do it. Of course, I'll be dead by the time you're reading this, so you can't ask anyway. Convenient of me, isn't it?) You should share with each other what it is that I've instructed you to do, but only when you are ready to do so.

Lastly, and this is very important, open a new envelope only when the previous envelope's instructions have been completed. After that, the new addressee can choose when to open his or her letter. No pushing allowed! I believe you'll know when you're ready, so trust each other.

That's it. Simple, isn't it?

Love,

Martha/Mimi

Neither of them knew what to say.

Noah reached inside the box and pulled out the envelope on top. "This is number one. And it's for you, Mom."

Brea took it with shaky hands. It was more than the letter. Noah hadn't said this much to her for several months. It was nice and scary at the same time. She was hopeful but afraid it wouldn't last.

She couldn't open the letter yet. She wanted to be alone when she did, not sure what to expect or what emotions might come pouring forth. She held the letter close, even furtively bringing it up to her nose so she could smell Martha's comforting scent.

Noah was holding the box, examining it from various sides, apparently fighting the temptation to riffle through all the envelopes. Suddenly he put the lid on and flipped it upside down.

"Noah!" Brea gasped.

"It's okay. They're numbered." He was staring intently at the bottom of the box. "Did you see this before?"

"See what?"

"This newspaper clipping. It's stuck to the bottom of the box. I saw the edge of it poking out on the side. But it's only part of a clipping."

"Well, I found the box stuck to a shelf in Martha's closet. The article must have been underneath, lining the shelf." It seemed a simple explanation to her, a happenstance easily dismissed.

"Can you show me?"

"Show you what?"

"Where you found the box, so I can see if there's more of this newspaper article. The middle of it is torn, but the other edges are neatly cut. It's not some random newspaper piece. Mimi deliberately saved this."

"Sure, I guess." It seemed inconsequential compared to the stack of envelopes inside the box and the one she was clutching in her hand, but there was no harm in bothering her parents one more time today.

Noah climbed the step ladder this time while Brea, Lizzie, and Earl watched from below. "Anything?"

Noah didn't respond right away. He was busy searching the shelf front to back. Dejected, he climbed down the ladder and turned to sit on a lower rung. "Nothing. Thanks for the flashlight, Grandpa."

"Sure. Sorry there wasn't anything there. I guess you'll have to solve your mystery with what you have."

"Yeah, I guess so."

"Have you two eaten yet?" Lizzie said. "Since we don't have a kitchen to speak of, we grabbed Indian takeout. There are leftovers in the fridge, if you want them. But you'll probably want to take them home to warm up. Our microwave is a little awkward to use." They had followed her to the kitchen, and she was pointing to where their microwave sat on the floor in the corner. "And then, of course, the seating situation isn't ideal." Two folding chairs sat on either side of the card table Lizzie and Earl had been sitting at earlier in the day.

"No, we haven't eaten. That would be great."

. . .

Brea busied herself with eating, recognizing her growling stomach—and her desire to put off opening the envelope from Martha. Unsure what it might contain, she kept glancing at it out of the corner of her eye where she'd left it on her kitchen counter.

Noah, however, was engrossed in deciphering what he could of the newspaper clipping. Upon returning home, he'd dumped out the envelopes and upturned Martha's box on the kitchen table directly under the light to see it more clearly.

"It mentions George Harrison. His name is circled. Do you think this is about the Beatles, Mom?"

Distracted, Brea didn't respond before Noah answered his own question. "No, it isn't. This mentions 1918. It calls George the Hero of Viborgne. What's Viborgne? Here, this is everything I can read:

> *… honored George Harrison, long-time resident of Summerhill. Various neighbors, friends, and family took their turns paying tribute to the man known as, "The Hero of Viborgne." Mr. Harrison is uncomfortable with the moniker. "That was a long time ago. I wasn't a hero. The men who died, they're the real heroes," he said.*
>
> *Dragging the story out of him isn't easy, but those who have known him longest fill in the details when he demurs. In 1918, …*

Noah set down the box. "That's it, Mom. Who was this guy? What do you think he did? Any idea why Mimi would save this?"

"I don't know." She viewed the article as a red herring, taking his focus away from the real meaning behind Martha's gift, and it annoyed her. It shouldn't have, but it did. One glance toward the backyard told her why. With only the light from the kitchen stretching into the yard, she could just make out a branch or two of the broken tree. She was more concerned with what that might mean, oblivious to the opportunity to talk with Noah that had just presented itself.

ENVELOPE #1

The new day brought new opportunities and plenty of time to think. Brea spent much of her day in the backyard. Her work could wait. Mr. Charles had cleaned up the apple tree nicely, but she felt the need to tend to flower beds, the other apple trees, the lawn—anything that kept her close to her tree.

By the time Noah returned from school, she had formulated a plan. She wanted to recapture what she and Noah had always had—a closeness, a willingness to talk to each other. She was not going to have a broken life and a broken son! That thought burned inside her.

It would be okay if he didn't share everything with her. What she wanted was for him to share enough that she knew not to worry. Paul had left his parents behind for a time, and she was going to fight to ensure the sins of the father were not repeated with the son.

Brea was waiting for him in the kitchen when school was over. She had a plate of nachos all ready to pop into the microwave. "Hi, Noah. How was your day?"

"Fine."

"Would you like some nachos?"

His "Sure" was accompanied by a small smile.

When Noah was halfway through his nacho plate, Brea pulled up a chair beside him. "Noah, I've been thinking. School's almost over. Why don't we take a vacation?"

Noah nodded while he finished his bite. "To see Grandma and Grandpa Caste? I mean, since Grandma and Grandpa Roberts are next door now?"

"Not exactly."

"Oh, taking a trip with one of them then?"

Over the years, that had been the nature of their vacations—off to see a set of grandparents or dragging grandparents off with them somewhere. But this time, Brea wanted to spend one-on-one time with Noah. Grandparents, wonderful as they were, would get in the way.

"I was thinking it was high time we took a vacation with just the two of us."

Noah shrugged. "Whatever." He put his now empty plate in the sink and pulled a notecard out of his pocket.

"What's that?"

He didn't hesitate to show it to her. He'd written "George Harrison" on one line and "Hero of Viborgne" on the next. "I can't find anything about this. During lunch at school, I googled it on my phone. 'George Harrison' just brings up the Beatle, so that's a waste. But I figured trying 'Hero of Viborgne' would tell me something. I found Viborgne, but nothing about a hero, literally nothing!" He was shaking his head as he left the kitchen to head upstairs to his room.

In frustration, Brea followed him. "Noah, are you listening to me?"

He spun to face her. "Are you listening to *me*?"

With a humph, Brea said, "Yes and no. I'm trying to. You're stuck on this old newspaper article that has no meaning. But you don't tell me anything about what's going on in your life, who your friends are, what actually matters to you. You don't tell me much, so excuse me if I'm not listening. There isn't much to listen to." She regretted her tone and her words as soon as they left her lips, but it was too late to take them back. "I'm sorry. That was too harsh. I'm … I guess I'm hypersensitive to secrets being kept from me."

Noah responded with a blank stare but no words.

"A trip, Noah. Would you like to take a trip together? That's all I want to know right now."

He stared at her for a long time before replying. "Okay, sure. To Europe, to Viborgne. I found it on the map. It's in France. I want to go to Europe to figure out this *meaningless* article." He spat the last two words in her face.

"You're kidding, right?"

While he held her gaze, his angry face relaxed slightly. "No, I'm not kidding. This matters to me, even if it doesn't to you. I want to go to Europe." Then he shrugged and, instead of going upstairs, went to the garage door. "I'm off to a friend's house. I'll be home in time for dinner." Sarcastically he added, "if you want to eat *together*."

Brea watched him tear off on his bike. The hole in her heart told her she'd deserved his words. Why did this have to be so hard? Where had her sweet, little boy gone?

It was only last year when they'd decided to build a Rube Goldberg machine together—the kind of chain reaction course that makes its way onto YouTube. He'd been twelve at the time, a double-digit age yet, significantly, not a teenager. It had taken them days to set up and took up most of their home's first floor—a mistake they realized the first evening at dinnertime when they discovered their course blocked the oven, dishwasher, and half the lower cupboards. Laughing at their short-sightedness, they went to the store for paper plates and cups then took turns choosing where to buy dinner for four nights—until the final reveal of their machine.

"Wow," was all Brea could say when they were done.

"I know, right?" They'd stared at their handiwork, afraid to move or even breathe deeply. Twice they inadvertently set one stage or another into motion, and only through quick thinking stopped the entire thing from prematurely going off.

"Hey, let's get Mimi!"

"Great idea. She'll love it!"

It had been a challenge to find a place for Martha to sit where she could watch the action as it passed by. She was growing feeble, but denial of her declining health was easy since the twinkle in her eye was as bright as ever.

"Mimi, do you want to do the honors?"

"I'd love to, Noah. Are you ready?"

Brea and Noah both had phones ready to record the action. "Yes, go!"

Martha knocked over the first domino. They all watched in awe as rows of dominos led to ping pong balls rolling down ramps leading to matchbox cars gliding across tracks that triggered strings that turned on fans, sending an umbrella scurrying to set another object in motion and then another.

Laughing with delight, they watched it to the end. It only misfired twice, but with a little nudge, it was soon back on track. It traveled through the kitchen, living room, hallways, family room, and back into the kitchen.

"I loved that!" Martha was cheering as much as they were.

Sitting down to watch their videos, Brea and Noah were surprised by more than their accomplishment—Martha was in every shot. "Mimi, you followed us from room to room! How did you manage that?"

She chuckled. "When it's important, I can be pretty speedy. I was just worried I'd set something off I wasn't supposed to. I didn't want to ruin anything."

Brea embraced her. "You could never ruin anything. Honestly, you make everything better."

. . .

Now, a year later, Brea needed someone or something to make everything better. All she'd accomplished so far with Noah was to add insult to injury. Her "brilliant" efforts to come together had instead driven a further wedge between them.

She collapsed into a chair in her living room. She was all for the kid having friends, but friends she knew. She'd even settle for simply knowing what they were doing together.

Sighing, she put her hands in her pockets. Her fingers touched the envelope she'd stuffed there. After dropping Noah off at school that morning, she'd opened the letter from Martha. And then she'd cancelled her lunch with Amy. The instructions Martha had given her seemed simple and straight-forward, but they weighed heavily in the pit of her stomach. Knowing Martha, they were deeper than first appeared. And if that was the case, certainly they would be harder to carry out than she initially thought.

All that made her realize she wasn't ready to face Amy over lunch. She'd sworn long ago not to hide things from Amy—her emotions, her struggles, her joys. Over lunch, Amy would look her in the eye, and she'd have no choice but to spill everything—the tree, how its damage heightened her concerns about Noah, probably in a completely irrational way, and the letter and its instructions that she didn't understand yet. How could she share with Amy what she hadn't yet processed herself? That thinking was dangerous, and she knew it. So, to make herself feel better, she merely postponed lunch for a day.

Giving herself twenty-four hours to come to grips with these latest events was a blessing and a curse. It could motivate her to pull her thoughts together, to not wallow. But in reality, she didn't know how to process things enough to talk them over with Amy, let alone deal with any of them. And now she'd given herself a deadline that loomed heavily over her. So, she'd gone out and worked in the yard instead, postponing and ignoring any and all concerns in her life—other than babysitting the tree.

Now, holding the envelope in her hands, she couldn't ignore it any longer. Taking the letter out of the envelope once again, Brea caught Martha's scent. She flattened the paper on her knees. It was a simple instruction written in Martha's beautiful yet shaky script: *Do something Noah wants to do that you don't.*

A trip to Europe? How could Martha have known it would play out like this? She shook that thought from her head. Obviously, she didn't know. Martha probably meant something like taking Noah to an amusement park or the new Asian fusion restaurant in town. She could do that. It wouldn't be much of a sacrifice on her part, simply a day out of her life.

Sacrifice. Was she willing to sacrifice for Noah? As a mother, she'd been doing that most of his life, hadn't she? Yet, even though she didn't want to admit it, she knew in her heart of hearts something that "wouldn't be much of a sacrifice" was not what Martha had in mind. That was the crux of what had bothered her that morning. She needed to dig deeper, and she knew it.

Everything about this scared her. Europe may be the dream vacation spot for many people, and maybe when she was younger Brea could have embraced the thought of it. But losing her husband so early forced her to put down roots for the sake of her infant son and their future. Stability was what she craved for Noah, for herself. Those roots had grown deep since that time.

It's why they only went on vacations to grandparents or with grandparents. Inviting Noah to take a trip with just the two of them was a leap, in and of itself. But it was offered in an effort to gain the Noah she knew back, to put stability back into her life.

How could she go to Europe where she didn't speak the languages they would encounter? She didn't know the money or the customs or how to order a taxi or how to know they were going the right direction or how to board a train or … The thoughts overwhelmed her. Going to Europe was definitely something she didn't want to do.

The paper from Martha slipped from her hand. It landed on the ground, face up. *Do something Noah wants to do that you don't.* Europe fit the bill to a tee, but there had to be another option.

GRAVESTONE

Brea played with the almond chicken salad in front of her. Amy's mother-in-law had offered to take Lia, so their lunch ended up being the two of them. Amy was buttering a roll and rattling off the latest exploits of D and D and Lia.

The interaction of siblings was not something Brea could relate to. She was an only child, as was Noah. In both instances, the desire for more children had gone unfulfilled by circumstances beyond their control. What would never come to pass pricked at Brea's heart in vulnerable moments, driving her to focus too acutely on Noah. He was her one chance to get it right.

"Hey, are you listening to me?"

"Um, sure. Lia and the Rice Krispies. How long did that take to clean up?"

"Oh, I made D and D help Lia since they're the ones who put her up to it in the first place."

Brea laughed lightly. She knew her façade wouldn't hold up much longer.

"Hey, this food is delicious. I hadn't tried this place before."

"Why do you think I suggested it?" Amy was notorious for her dislike of cooking. Her husband, Spencer, had started learning to cook as a defense mechanism. "Just so you know, they offer takeout and have lots of kid-friendly options."

"Gee. It's almost like you know me."

"Yeah, almost."

"And it's almost like I know you're stalling." Amy's raised eyebrow spoke volumes. "Are you going to tell me on your own, or do I need to drag it out of you?"

Brea's shoulders relaxed. The thought of sharing what she was holding in was surprisingly appealing. "It's Noah." She took a deep breath before plunging in. "He wants to go to Europe."

"By himself?" Amy's voice rose in surprise.

"No. The two of us."

"Oh, that's better. In fact, that's great! Are you worried about the cost?"

"No," She shook her head in frustration. "No, the cost isn't a problem."

"Well, what then? Why were you so reluctant to tell me?"

"It's complicated. I'm worried about Noah. He's hiding things from me, and then Paul's tree got damaged, and–"

"Paul's tree? What happened to the apple tree?"

As Brea related the events and concerns of the last few days—about Noah, the tree, the envelopes, even her reluctance to travel to a foreign country—she felt her pulse slow and her breathing calm. She ended her tale by spreading Martha's note on the table between them.

To her relief, Amy didn't laugh or make light of Brea's concerns. "I know you—have known you for a long time. I've never had a teenager before, so I'm not experienced with that. However, I do know Noah. He's a good kid. So, while you're likely overreacting, it's possible you're nipping something in the bud."

Brea sighed. "That's what I'm worried about, the possibility."

"Based on my memory of being a teenager, there's a fine line to walk. If they're not doing anything wrong but you act like they are, you can alienate them. On the other hand, if they're in trouble and you ignore it, that can lead to all kinds of negative consequences, some of them life-long." She reached across the table to put her hand on Brea's. "I remember Paul's past issues. So,

I can understand how his apple tree being damaged would highlight that for you."

"Thank you for that validation. I thought I was going nuts, but it's just all too real."

"No. I get it. You have a right to be concerned, even though this is all relatively new with Noah. Of course, if he is up to no good and you catch him at it, you also may alienate him, the same as if he were on the up and up. The only good point being you could prevent a lot of heartache."

"So, what you're saying is there's no way for Noah and me to be on good terms at the end of this?"

Amy chuckled uncomfortably. "I did paint that bleak picture, didn't I? I told you I wasn't great with parenting a teenager." She shrugged.

They sat in silence for a few minutes, pondering the possible options.

"I'm not sure how you fix a broken tree," Amy mused quietly. Then her eyes flew open. "Hey, I know!"

"What? What can I do?"

"Take Noah to Europe."

"Really? Did you hear the part where I don't want to take him to Europe? He's gone off on this tangent about that old newspaper article. I need to pull him back from things like that, not indulge them."

Amy merely smiled at her, saying nothing. Finally, she tipped her head toward the paper open before them on the table: *Do something Noah wants to do that you don't.* When Brea didn't respond, she nodded more urgently, making a show of drawing her eyes down to Martha's written words.

"Oh, sheesh! How is that going to help? Honestly!"

"You already know the answer to that. You're the one who taught me that parenting isn't just about making rules and enforcing them. You've got to care about him and his interests, even if they're not your interests. You've always said, 'Limit the lectures but not the love.'

"Remember all the tee-ball games you insisted 'Auntie Amy' attend because Noah loved to see me there? And what about the behind-the-scenes zoo visit to see the tarantulas and the snakes up close. You hate those things. But you took Noah because you love him."

"Geez. Would you stop making so much sense?"

"And what was the result of those things? It's because of things like that you and Noah have been so close in the first place. Do you know what he told me after your zoo visit? He said, 'Mom doesn't like snakes, but she likes me. She loves me. That's why she's the best mom in the whole world.'"

"You're not playing fair." Brea attempted a dirty look then gave up. "Why do I even bother talking to you?"

With a wicked glint in her eye, Amy said, "So, when can I expect my first postcard to arrive?" Brea returned a glare.

Ignoring it, Amy continued, "You know, you'll get him all to yourself there. You'll need to depend on each other. And while you're doing that, you are going to have the time of your life building shared memories."

"You almost make me want to go," Brea said, shaking her head. "I better get home and get some work done if I'm going to end up taking all this time off."

"Good idea. And now you owe me one."

"I owe you one? You've done me a favor? I came here hoping you could help me find an alternative to this. And instead, you've pushed me headlong into it. Why in the world would I owe you one for that?"

"Because it's the right thing to do, and you knew it all along."

"You're insufferable when you're right."

. . .

Brea was in her office finishing the work she'd been unable to focus on that morning when Noah walked in from school. She closed her laptop and went to greet him.

Instead of the usual, "How was your day," with its typical and unsatisfactory answer, she said, "Noah, I haven't been very patient or understanding with you lately. I'm sorry for that."

His head came up, and he met her eyes. He said nothing but acknowledged her apology with a slight nod.

She resisted the urge to ruffle his hair. "Before dinner, I was thinking of visiting Martha's grave. I miss her. Would you like to go with me?"

Noah looked at her without moving. Softly, he said, "I miss her too."

She smiled wistfully back at him. "Then, shall we go?"

. . .

Driving to the cemetery in silence, Brea thought of her relationship with Martha. She'd been a friend and confidante, but she'd also been like an extra grandmother, someone who loved her unconditionally and supported her in every endeavor. And if that qualified her as an extra grandmother, she was the same for Noah. Brea glanced at Noah beside her. Smiling, she thought, *I don't see why we can't share the same extra grandmother.*

They had been to this cemetery many times to visit Paul's grave, but Martha was buried in a different corner of it. Brea and Noah had only visited her gravesite once—the day of her funeral. Noah had been a pallbearer, helping carry Martha's coffin to the spot next to her husband where she would be laid to rest.

The day was clear with a blue sky interrupted only by faint, wispy clouds. It took them just a few minutes to locate the slight rise where she was buried. The area was teeming with new growth, the grass thick and high. A gentle breeze teased the blades, the scent of a nearby freshly mown swath reaching them. White clover flowers popped their heads up above where her coffin resided.

"It's beautiful," Brea murmured.

Noah nodded. "It feels wrong that Mimi's not alive and part of it."

The headstone had been installed upon her husband's passing twenty-four years before, and Martha's name and birthdate were etched into the unforgiving stone next to his, a frozen monument to lives once lived. For two dozen years the half-empty marble on her side had waited for a confirmation of her final curtain call.

It was odd to see a headstone already in place at the time of her funeral. When Paul died, Brea had needed to wait for the headstone to be installed. But Martha's burial plot and headstone were already ready for her, waiting like an impatient timekeeper.

She shouldn't have felt that way since Martha had lived almost an entire century. But any time she passed would have seemed too soon. The holes in Brea's and Noah's hearts bore that out.

On this day, they had stopped at the grocery store and bought a small bouquet of flowers in a slender vase. Noah silently held it on his lap on the way. Now he gently placed it in front of Martha's name then sat down cross-legged in front of it.

Brea moved up beside him, reading the engraved name over his shoulder. With a choked-off sob, she noted the fresh cuts in the marble. The date of Martha's exit from mortality stared back at them. Crouching, Brea traced the hollowed-out letters and numbers with her finger. "It's so final being written in stone like this," she said softly.

Noah reached out and quietly mimicked his mother's actions, tenderly tracing her name, Martha. "Mom?" It came out as a barely audible whisper. "Mom?" more clearly this time.

"What, Noah?"

"What's that?" He was pointing at the headstone.

"What's what?"

"Her name." Across the top of the headstone in capital letters was FEREDAY.

"Her name? Since they shared the same last name, they carve it once across the top for both of them." Brea was puzzled by Noah's confusion.

"I know that. I mean the other name."

Brea scanned the headstone to see what had caught his attention. Martha's side of the marker read:

Beloved Wife and Mother
Martha Harrison

She read that far and stopped. "Martha Harrison?"

"Yes! Her maiden name. It was Harrison. Do you think George Harrison is related to her?"

"It's not that unusual of a name, but it's certainly possible. Do the math to see what might fit."

"What math?"

"Figure it out from the article. When was George alive?"

"The article mentioned the year 1918. That was most likely when he became the Hero of Viborgne."

"Where did you say Viborgne was?"

"France."

"That sounds like World War I. When was Martha born?" They both abruptly turned to the headstone. Together they said, "1921."

"He could have been her dad or her uncle," Noah exclaimed with triumph.

"Yes. Although, George and Harrison are common enough names," Brea added, but Noah didn't hear her.

"Do you have paper and a pencil? I want to write all this down."

From her purse-of-all-trades, Brea easily produced the writing materials for Noah. Then she sat back to observe while Noah eagerly copied down names and dates. A peace washed over her. Even in death Martha was working her magic—on both of them.

At times when Brea had been caught up in the minutiae of parenting—checking assignments, driving Noah to appointments and practices, monitoring teeth brushing and the eating of vegetables—Martha had fostered Noah's curiosity, in the process reminding Brea to do the same. It was actually because of Martha they had gone behind the scenes at the zoo to see the snakes and other creepy crawlies.

"Do you want to go with us?" Brea had asked.

"No, I'm a little tired. I don't think I'm up to it today."

Brea knew it was an excuse. Initially, she assumed it was because Martha wasn't fond of snakes, but soon realized that view was merely based on her own distaste of the slithering beasts. The real reason then became obvious. Martha was letting Brea take all the credit for fostering young Noah's interest in the world around him. A wistful smile played on her lips—Martha, always unselfish Martha. It was just one of many such examples she could recall.

"Noah." He didn't hear her, his attention still riveted on the stone in front of him. "Noah."

Surprised, he turned. "Yes?"

"I opened the first envelope. It said … well, Martha always did know best. If you want to go to Europe, we can go."

His eyes grew wide. "You mean it? We can go?" He jumped up, threw a fist-pump in the air while whooping and hollering. "Thank you, Mom! Thank you so much!" He reached for her hand, pulled her up, swinging her around in a carefree dance. He tipped his head back and let out a joyous, carefree laugh.

Brea grinned. Once again Martha was letting her take all the credit.

EUROPE

On the way home, Brea formulated a plan. First, take care of dinner, then attack the logistics of a trip. "Noah, let's order pizza. Would you like some wings to go with it?" Once they made their choices, Noah placed an order on his phone. They would arrive home shortly before their dinner did.

"What's your homework situation like?"

"I've got math, but I finished most of it in class. It shouldn't take more than a few minutes. I have a couple projects coming up, but they don't need to be done today."

"Okay. What about the rest of the year? We could try to leave for Europe right after school's out. I'm guessing the sooner we get going, the better. That way maybe we can miss the biggest wave of tourists. Do you think you can get ready to leave and handle finals at the same time? If not, we could wait a week."

"Mom, there's only a few weeks left. The last week is usually just time to goof off. We could try to leave early, before school's out."

"Would you feel bad leaving your friends? Skipping that last week?"

"No. It wouldn't matter." He sounded distracted. "I'll look over what schoolwork I have left."

Brea turned at his tone, but seeing nothing, shrugged and turned back to driving.

. . .

While Brea checked on flights and vacation rentals, Noah disappeared into his room. By the time their pizza and wings arrived, she had a couple possible itineraries, depending on when Noah could get away from school.

"So, Noah, what did you figure out? When do you want to leave?"

"As soon as possible, honestly. When I finish the projects I'm working on, I'm basically done with most of my classes. In math, we only have two assignments left. And I'm almost done with my last science experiment. That just leaves my finals. I'll bet I can get my teachers to let me take my finals early or maybe skip them altogether since I'm pulling mostly A's."

"That's great. Do you want me to talk to your teachers?"

"No. I'll do it."

"Okay. Then I'll check with the office about you missing the last week or so of school. It shouldn't be a problem. I think you've only had one absence all school year–"

"For Mimi's funeral," he finished for her. Brea nodded. They ate their meal in silence, each lost in their own thoughts.

As they cleaned up and put the leftovers away, Noah tapped his mom on the arm. She started at the once familiar touch. "Mom, will you call Mimi's kids to ask about George Harrison for me?"

"Sure." It was the first favor he had directly asked her for in a long time. Yes, he wanted to go to Europe, but that was merely in response to her invitation to take a trip somewhere. "Of course I will," she quickly added.

Brea had Susan's number. She was Martha's oldest child, and she lived nearby. They had exchanged phone numbers once Martha turned 90, just in case.

She opened her phone to call when Noah again touched her on the arm. "I googled Viborgne and World War I. I should have made that connection before, but I guess I didn't think about it." He shrugged then added sheepishly, "Thanks for the idea." He gave her a faint smile and continued, "Anyway, I knew Viborgne was in France. I didn't find it listed in any World War I activity, but it's close to Château-Thierry. A lot happened there. So, I'm guessing some of it could have easily spilled over into Viborgne. It's a pretty small town, from what I can tell."

She raised her eyebrows. "So, I'm guessing that's what was on your mind on the way home?"

He nodded and couldn't help but smile.

Brea automatically ruffled his hair before realizing what she was doing and pulled back. Only Noah didn't mind. He hadn't stiffened or given her even the slightest grimace.

. . .

Susan picked up promptly. "Hi, Brea. How are you doing? How's the house shaping up for your parents?"

"It's going great. You won't recognize the place." She gasped slightly. "Oh … I didn't …"

"No. It's okay. My mother was a very old woman, which makes me a moderately old woman. I took pictures of the place before we sold it. I didn't expect it to remain unchanged."

Brea breathed a sigh of relief. "That's good."

"All the same, I've resisted the urge to drive by the place. It probably looks the same on the outside, but it's still so odd to think that Mom's not sitting inside with a plate of warm muffins waiting for me or one of my kids."

"I know what you mean. I see the house every day. It was probably a solid two months before its sight didn't make me cry." Brea shook her head then spotted Noah and shifted the conversation.

"Susan, I actually have a specific question I called about. I was wandering around your mom's house and found a box in the top of her bedroom closet. It was addressed to me and Noah. You know your mom, always trying to do some good. Anyway, there was a newspaper article stuck to the bottom of it, or at least a portion of a clipping. It talks about George Harrison, and today we went to the cemetery and realized your mother's maiden name was Harrison. So, is George–"

"George was my grandpa, Mom's dad."

"Cool!" She gave Noah a thumbs up. "Did he serve in World War I; do you know?"

"I think so, but I don't remember him, or anyone for that matter, ever talking about it."

"Did you ever hear anything about Viborgne or the Hero of Viborgne?"

"No, that doesn't sound familiar. What is it?"

"That's just it. We haven't the faintest idea."

· · ·

Noah grew thoughtful once Brea repeated the conversation to him. "Hmm. I'm glad we know who he is, but I thought she might be able to tell us more. You'd think his family would know if he was a hero."

"True, but we don't always share our histories. We assume people know things, or we just don't get around to telling our stories." Brea shrugged. "Do you still want to go to Viborgne?"

"Yes! Of course I do." His tone held a challenge.

"All right," she said, throwing up her arms. "I simply meant—even if we can't solve the mystery or find any answers?"

"We'll find answers," he said in frustration before storming off.

"Oh, Noah, I sure hope so. I want to find answers too," she said to herself.

· · ·

Brea returned to her task at hand, losing track of time while searching for possible things they could do on a trip to Europe. The choices were staggering. France alone presented plenty of options, but other countries nearby beckoned as well. She'd have to find a way to ferret out what Noah would like to do. Since they were taking a trip all the way to Europe, they might as well make the most of it.

Despite stomping off, Noah had softened and was talking to her, for which she was relieved and grateful, but she could tell he was still on a razor's edge. She would need to tread carefully.

When she went upstairs to bed, Noah's door was open. She took a chance and poked her head in. "Hi." He looked up, his face impassive. She took that as a positive sign. "We can talk more tomorrow, but I have some options for

Europe. I figured as long as we're going, we may as well pack our schedule with things we'd like to see."

He nodded slightly. She turned to go, when he said, "Mom?"

"Yes?"

"France is what I care about." He had a hard glint in his eye, but when he spoke, his tone was gentle. "Maybe we'll find answers there and maybe we won't, but I want to try. We have to try." His voice rose with the last words.

"Okay, Noah. We will. I promise."

His shoulders visibly relaxed. "Mom, I understand there are no guarantees in life. Dad died just when he decided to do the right thing—actually because of it. I wish he was still alive, but I'm glad he didn't go on doing the wrong thing."

When did he get to be so wise? Brea wondered.

"I know things don't always work out the way we want them to," Noah continued, "but even though I can't always pick the outcome, I can try to influence it." He shrugged. "Learning about George Harrison is important to me. I can't explain it, it just is. I have to know what happened."

"Okay," Brea said, but inwardly her stomach churned. He was obsessing over George Harrison. It set off a whole array of alarm bells in her head. It was when Paul got caught up in one idea that he lost sight of the big picture. He became oblivious to what he was really involved with. That was when his real trouble started.

Without either of them realizing it, the night outside had grown black and ominous. An unexpected crack of thunder made them both jump. Brea had to catch her breath, and it jumbled her thoughts. She glanced at Noah, still so young and yet on the verge of manhood. Finding the story behind a hero seemed safe enough, didn't it? But the thought that she didn't know for sure unsettled her.

BENJAMIN ROBERTS

For the next couple days, both Noah and Brea found themselves caught up in a flurry of activity, each trying to finish things that would allow them to take off soon and for who knows how long. But even with all the preparation for their trip, Brea had made no reservations or definite itinerary. She hadn't even bought plane tickets. She didn't want to do that without Noah's input, and he had become uncommunicative once again.

Noah wasn't sullen or touchy like he'd been of late, but he was lost in his own thoughts. Any time Brea attempted to ask more than, "How was your day?" it was as if a heavy door shut in her face with Noah hiding behind it.

So, she made preparations without making plans, not sure what else to do. She tried broaching the topic with, "Noah, when we go to Europe–," only to be cut off before she could finish.

"Viborgne, Mom. You know that's where I want to go."

"I know. We will, but–"

"But nothing." And he would disappear into his room without another word.

. . .

Friday afternoon rolled around. Now that Grandma and Grandpa lived next door, they often came over for a Family Fun Night on Fridays. It typically consisted of takeout or delivery for dinner followed by movies or games.

"Noah, are you up for spending the evening with Grandma and Grandpa, or … do you want to get together with your friends?" She didn't know much about those friends, but she didn't want to alienate Noah, likely pushing him away from herself and into those friends' hands instead. It was a fine line to walk.

He only hesitated briefly before saying, "Grandma and Grandpa would be fine."

"What should we order for dinner?"

He often had strong opinions about the food, but this time he shrugged. "Surprise me," he said then took off for his room.

When Brea got home later with fried chicken from one of their favorite local places, Noah was setting up a game in the family room. He already had paper plates and drinks laid out on the kitchen table.

"Thanks, Noah." Maybe she'd been misreading him, that he wasn't angry at the world just wrapped up in his thoughts about it. Of course, that had been one of her concerns all along, hadn't it?

"Sure. No problem."

"I honked at your grandpa when I pulled in. He was out in his yard. I'm guessing they'll be here in a minute."

"Okay. Cool." He almost smiled.

Taking a chance, Brea said, "Noah, I need to make reservations, but I want your input. Viborgne is obviously the highlight," then she was quick to add, "but we need to decide what else we want to do or where we might want to go."

"Oh, I hadn't thought about that."

A knock sounded followed by the opening of their front door. Earl and Lizzie burst into the family room a moment later with big grins. "Hey, how's our favorite grandson?"

"Hi, Grandma. Hi, Grandpa."

Dinner was soon underway with an easy banter around the kitchen table. As they were finishing the last of it, Noah asked, "Grandpa, Grandma, were your dads in World War I?"

Lizzie chuckled gently. "Oh, no. That was too long ago."

"But mine did serve in World War II," Earl added.

"Oh. Then what about his dad, your grandpa?"

"Hmm. Yes, he did. He was Italian, still in Italy at the time. So, he fought in it, lived during it, endured it—in more ways than most Americans."

"Wow. Where did he fight?"

"I have no idea."

"When did he come to America?"

"I'm not sure. My dad was born here, so it had to have been before that."

This was history Brea had never heard before. She was intrigued. "Dad, are you talking about your Grandpa Roberts?"

"Yes, Benjamin Roberts."

"He was Italian? Roberts doesn't sound Italian at all." Noah's interest was waning but Brea's imagination was piqued.

"No, it's not. He changed his name when he came here to something that sounded more American."

"Do you know what he changed it from?"

"I'm sorry. I don't."

· · ·

The next morning, Brea rose early, but she let Noah sleep in. Her parents had stayed late playing games. Once they left, Brea and Noah had both gone straight to bed. She hadn't broached the topic of their trip and where they wanted to go again. Hopefully, Noah would be in a good mood when he woke up. She wanted to cement their plans.

A light tap on the front door interrupted her thoughts. "Hi, Dad. You're up and about early."

"Yeah, I was thinking about my grandpa last night."

"Your grandpa?"

"Yes, Benjamin Roberts."

"Oh, right." Intrigued as she'd been, he had slipped her mind.

"So, I searched through our boxes and found this." He held out a large book that Brea hadn't noticed tucked under his arm.

"What is it?" Then a light went on. "Oh! Is that a family Bible?"

"It is."

Brea ushered him in, and he gently laid the Bible on her kitchen table. He opened the front cover. Inked-in entries listed names and birthdates.

"This is amazing, Dad."

"I'm afraid this doesn't have as much information as some. It's an English language Bible, so I'm guessing Benjamin bought it once he came to America. His name is at the top."

Brea traced the lettering of his name: Beniamino. "Now that sounds Italian." The Beniamino had been crossed out, and underneath it was written Benjamin Roberts. "His changed name must have been new to him. You know, old habits die hard. It's too bad he didn't write his Italian last name too."

"I agree. He didn't list his parent's names either, which is too bad. But his birthdate is recorded."

In different colored ink was written *23 February 1895 Orvieto, Italy.* "It appears he added this later, maybe realizing the importance of recording vital information in a family Bible."

Her father chuckled. "No, I think my grandma realized the importance of that. Look. Her name, Hazel Shepherd, is written on the line below in the same color ink and the same handwriting as Benjamin's birthdate."

Sure enough, the handwriting matched. "Dad, I'll bet their marriage date 10 April 1920 was written by Hazel too. See how the 2 in 1920 has the same loops as the 2 in the 23 of his birthdate? The birth of their first child, your dad, was recorded later. It's the same handwriting but a different pen. Walter Roberts 8 July 1921."

Earl Roberts left the Bible in his daughter's care and bid her farewell. She gently carried it into her office.

A couple hours later, Noah, rubbing the sleep out of his eyes, discovered his mother retrieving a piece of paper from her printer. "Morning, Mom."

"Good morning, Noah. Come take a look at this." She carefully showed him the Bible. "And I just found his record from Ellis Island. See? Here's Benjamin Roberts listed." She pointed to his name on the page she'd printed out. "His last permanent address was Vicenza, Italy. He came here to America in May 1919, shortly after the war."

Noah nodded, showing only mild interest.

"Noah, we need to finalize our plans so I can buy tickets and make reservations. What would you think of tacking on Italy? I'd like to learn more about Beniamino, if I can."

He shrugged in answer. "Sure, why not?" He turned toward the kitchen to find some breakfast, then turned back to face his mom. "But, let's do Italy first and France second."

"Okay. But, why?"

"I need more time to do research. There's got to be more to learn. Since I'll only have one shot at Viborgne, I have to get it right the first time."

HEROES

It was surprising how quickly all the pieces could come together. Brea and Noah already owned passports since they made occasional jaunts into Canada with each set of grandparents. The flights they were interested in were available—at a cost. Finding a combination of vacation rentals and hotel rooms completed the basics of what they needed.

They would be flying into Rome after an all-night flight. Then the trip would be a combination of playing tourist and tracking down information about Benjamin Roberts or George Harrison. Finding what they were looking for was another matter. Brea knew it wouldn't be as simple as all that, and she was hoping Noah knew that too.

In the end, they left a few days before school was out. Noah was alternating between talkative and secretive, but Brea saw that as better than all secretive. So, she was eager to get started and not lose any momentum. Noah honestly didn't seem to mind missing the final days of school, which surprised her a little, despite it being his idea. But she didn't give it much thought, choosing simply to be grateful.

As Noah dozed during their flight, Brea noticed he'd been doodling in a notebook. Most of it related to the Hero of Viborgne. His fascination with this hero still mystified her.

Hero was an interesting word. Paul had been hailed a hero when he died. He was and he wasn't—it all depended on your definition. He had gotten caught up in the possibility of exploiting credit card machines by inserting a programming glitch and shared that idea with a friend who brought in another accomplice. It wasn't until he figured out he could swindle the machines at will that the moral implications of it hit him. Those moral quandaries coincided with having a new baby in the house—Noah.

Wanting to be a good father and a good man, Paul had tried to back out of the criminal scheme but his partners would have none of it, even threatening Brea and Noah's lives. So, he sabotaged the efforts instead. That alone might qualify him as a hero, but that had to be balanced with the fact that he set the whole thing in motion in the first place.

The real heroic act happened when one of his accomplices pointed a gun at an old man, a loose end. When he fired, Paul jumped in the way, taking the bullet that would have ended the old man's life, ending Paul's life instead. He was the hero who saved the day after almost ruining it. He was a hero for fixing his own mistakes.

Brea had determined to share with Noah the story of his father, warts and all. And she had—at first in broad brush strokes then with more detail as Noah grew and was capable of understanding more nuance. She was kind in her treatment of Paul without being dishonest. But they hadn't talked about him as much lately. It's not as if the story changed any, and Noah already knew all the details.

Occasionally Paul's parents would remember a new childhood story to share. It might be triggered by something they saw on a trip or while watching an old movie. They would pull Noah close and tell him as much as they could remember or call him on the phone to recount it. But even those stories had diminished lately.

Brea gently brushed Noah's hair off his face. Asleep, he was her little boy again—the one who would climb into her bed after a nightmare, the one who excitedly brought her every lost tooth, the one who wiped her tears when she cried at a sad movie. He was her everything. She slipped off into slumber next to him with a wistful smile upon her face.

. . .

Rome came at them like a firehose. People were everywhere, talking in a rush with words neither of them understood and gestures they could only guess at interpreting. They breathed a sigh of relief when someone spoke directly to them and quickly understood the need to switch to English. The immigration and customs official was fluent in English and very kind. The first taxi driver they approached was neither. Thankfully, the second one had passable English and a friendly smile, so they hopped into his car. They couldn't follow all the turns he was taking, but they trusted him—as if they had another choice. Before long, he dropped them off at a little bungalow outside the center of Rome yet very much in the middle of a culture shock for Brea and Noah.

"This is great!" Noah said even before Concetta, their short, dynamic host, ushered them inside their vacation rental.

Brea was overwhelmed. It *was* incredible, but it was completely out of her comfort zone. "I can't believe we're doing this," she mumbled to herself.

"Come, come." Concetta eagerly showed them the two bedrooms, the small kitchen, and then burst open the back door with a flourish to reveal a charming patio. Brea and Noah had seen pictures of it in the listing, but those photos did not do it justice.

Terracotta planters greeted them filled with red roses and purple hyacinths, whose fragrances swirled in the warm air, drawing Brea and Noah further outside. A small hedge surrounded the stone patio, and a table occupied the center with a large, white umbrella shading it. Grape vines climbing a trellis completed the peaceful scene. "This is beautiful! Did you plant all these?"

Concetta beamed and nodded. "Me and *mio marito*, my husband."

"His name is Marito?" Brea asked.

Concetta laughed. "No. *Marito* means 'husband.' His name is Franco."

Concetta had thoughtfully stocked staples in the fridge and cupboards while pointing out a grocery store across the street. She left them with a smile and a phone number in case they needed anything during their stay.

It was afternoon by then. Tired yet excited, they opted to walk around the surrounding neighborhood. They bought groceries, even managing the foreign money, discovered a delightful restaurant to try later, and met several friendly dogs and their owners.

After putting groceries away, they unpacked. It didn't take long. The last item Brea unpacked took up an inordinate amount of space in her luggage—Martha's box. She had suggested to Noah they put the envelopes in a zippered, plastic bag, but his face fell as soon as she suggested it. "Or maybe I could fit the whole box in my suitcase, in case you want the article handy." Noah shrugged in response, but the relief he registered told Brea she'd made an important recovery. Even though not much of the article existed and what did exist was committed to his memory, having the article itself was important to him.

"We made it. I can't believe we're here." Brea sat down on the couch next to Noah and put the box between them. "You thanked me for letting us come on this trip, but you know it's Martha's doing, don't you?" She lifted the lid off the box and picked up envelope #1 that she'd opened. "I put this back in the box. It somehow just belongs here."

He took it from her, opened it and read, *Do something Noah wants to do that you don't.* He grinned at his mom. "You didn't tell me specifically what it said before, but I got the idea."

"I figured as much. This is crazy being here, but now that we're here, I'm thinking I could get used to all this. It's growing on me—the patio, the neighborhood, … and we haven't even seen any sights yet." She ruffled his hair, and he didn't object. "Do you think it still counts if this is now something I want to do too?"

He pretended to need time to think before answering, "Yeah, I guess so. I'll give you a pass this time."

"Thanks for your generosity—I think. Now, it's your turn. The next envelope is yours." She held up the box to him, but he didn't take it.

"Yep," he said casually, "when I'm ready."

It was part of the instructions from Martha, but Brea had to work to hide her disappointment. Without a word, she set the box down on the coffee table in front of them.

"So, when should we go to dinner?"

"Umm, I guess in a little bit?" But a few minutes later when they both started to nod off, Noah stood up straight. "If we plan to eat tonight, I think we need to go sooner rather than later."

The motion and the sound of his voice made Brea start. She shook the sleep out of her eyes. "You're right."

She grabbed her purse and they headed out. "I'm glad the restaurant's so close. If we had to ride in a cab, I think we'd be asleep before the car even started."

Noah nodded his agreement. "I am hungry, though."

"Well, that's a surprise."

. . .

Their hastily purchased guidebooks had informed them that eating was a much slower affair in Europe. Having been forewarned, the two of them were content to nibble on their cheese appetizer and watch the Italians around them while waiting for other parts of their meal to arrive.

"I don't understand a thing anyone's saying," Noah said, "but I love listening to them talk. It's crazy to think all those sounds have meaning. I think I heard the word 'pizza.' Other than that, it's kind of gibberish, but cool gibberish."

"That's probably not how I'd describe it, but I get what you're saying. It's such a pretty language. I wish I understood it." Brea did feel that way, but mostly she appreciated that Noah was talking freely.

They had managed ordering their dinner with a phrase book. If they'd been in the center of Rome, it's likely an English version of the menu would be available. But off the beaten path where they were was a different story.

Even still, they were curious to see if what they thought they ordered turned out to be what showed up. The cheese, fresh mozzarella, was tasty. When the pasta arrived, it looked just as promising. They had both ordered *amatriciana*. It had the appearance of spaghetti with marinara sauce, but the taste was quite different, surprisingly spicy and very delicious.

While they ate, Brea kept thinking of Martha's box. She wanted to know why Noah had been so reluctant to open the next envelope. She opened her mouth twice to ask him but shut it instead. The instructions from Martha said no pushing. It was as if Brea could hear Martha's voice in her head reminding her of that. It was almost certain Brea was the reason that particular instruction was given. Martha knew her all too well.

Struggling to leave it alone, Brea brought up a different topic. "Noah, tell me about the news clipping. Why is it so important to you?"

He set his fork down but didn't immediately respond. Brea went back to eating, thinking he wasn't going to answer when he surprised her by saying, "I'm not sure. I guess it's because of Mimi."

"Mimi? Martha? What do you mean?"

"She just meant a lot to me."

"I know. She was like a loving grandma to both of us."

"No, she wasn't. I mean, I know she loved me, but I didn't think of her as a grandma."

"Oh? I thought …"

"I know you did. I guess I wanted you to believe that. But really she was Switzerland."

"Switzerland?"

"Yes. She was neutral territory. She wasn't family. I mean, she was like family but not technically blood. So, she didn't have to sugar coat anything."

"Oh. Like what?"

"Dad."

It came out so quickly, so bluntly. Brea should have been taken aback, but she wasn't. She didn't want to admit it, but she knew she'd never be unbiased about Paul. She loved him too much not to be. When she'd first learned of his indiscretions, she'd been so stunned and not sure how to feel. But once she'd been able to forgive him, she started to see him in a different light. He was human and very fallible, but he'd been good in so many ways too. "I guess I understand that," she finally said.

"In my mind, he was an antihero more than a hero. Mimi taught me that word but then pointed out I had it wrong. He wasn't without his flaws, some glaring, but it wasn't his fault the others had guns and tried to shoot Mr. Walker. The credit card fraud was the only thing he set up, and he sabotaged that. Mimi taught me to be proud of him and not ashamed."

"Why didn't you talk to me about this? I could have–"

"No, you would have defended him, or, just the opposite, you'd feel like you let me down and try to make up for it. I needed someone unbiased. Mimi wasn't actually unbiased, but she was close. We talked about it for months.

Or at least Mimi listened while I talked about it for months before she said anything. And even then, she only gradually made her argument."

"I … I didn't know that."

Noah shrugged. "Our last conversation about it was the week before she died. It brought me to that final conclusion." He shook his head. "At least, I have to hope that was the final conclusion. I sometimes wonder if there was more she wanted to tell me, but she just ran out of time."

Brea gently laid a hand on top of his and wisely said nothing.

"The article about George Harrison feels like a missing link. Did Mimi know what made him a hero? Is that why she was able to talk to me about Dad? Or was it a mystery for her too? I don't know, but I have to find out. I feel I owe it to her, to her memory, or maybe I owe it to myself."

They were both silent for some time, the hubbub around them fading in their ears as they pondered what had passed between them.

"Mom?"

"Yes?"

"I have a question for you."

"What, Noah?" With his admission, she would happily answer anything—or so she thought.

"Why didn't you remarry?"

"What? Well, I … I never had the opportunity."

"That's not true. You dated, but you never gave any of them a chance. And then you turned down their dates until they stopped asking."

Her eyes flew open. He was more observant than she'd realized. But since when did he have the right to question such things? This conversation was not going in a direction she had any desire to entertain. She stared at Noah in shocked silence and shifted uncomfortably. The arrival of their next course saved her.

As their waiter left, Brea dove into the fish she had ordered even though she'd lost her appetite.

"I'm not the only one who doesn't talk, Mom," Noah said before deliberately picking up a forkful of food and stuffing it ungracefully into his mouth.

IT'S COMPLICATED

Returning to their apartment, Brea was full of regrets. The remainder of their dinner had taken place in silence. Their food was delicious, but neither of them finished what was in front of them.

Sinking into the couch, Brea spied Martha's box. The envelope on top gaped at her. She reached for it and opened it once again. *Do something Noah wants to do that you don't.* It came as a gut punch. She hadn't fulfilled it yet, but she could.

She didn't want to talk about her romantic life—or lack thereof. She didn't like thinking about it herself. And being accountable to a thirteen-year-old was an uncomfortable feeling.

The internal battle raged as she heard Noah getting ready for bed. If she waited any longer, the impact of her gift, her sacrifice, would be diminished. The moment was now.

Glancing down, she found Martha's note crumpled in her hands. Martha. Martha rarely steered her wrong.

Before she could change her mind, she called, "Noah, could you come here a moment, please?"

He came out of his bedroom to face her. The angry fire was gone from his eyes, but his face was inscrutable and he said nothing.

"If you're not too tired … No, let me try this again." She took a deep breath then plunged forward. "You were right. I haven't been open with you, and I should have been. It's wrong of me to expect transparency from you when I haven't been willing to give it in return. So, if you're not too tired, ask me anything you want. I promise to answer the best I can."

Noah raised his eyes skeptically, but when his mother didn't shy away from his questioning glance, a sly grin crept onto his face. "Is this a one-time thing? Or is this a forever thing?"

"Wow, give you an inch …" Her voice sounded stern, but she was grinning. "I suppose it's a forever thing, but I reserve the right to claim 'need to know.'"

He threw up his hands in surrender. "Okay."

Where they'd both been tired a moment before, an electricity buzzed between them now. "So … don't keep me waiting. What do you want to know?"

"What happened with you and men? How come you never had a serious boyfriend? You're still young and attractive. You're kind and loving. So, what's the deal, Mom?"

"Well, that's several questions, but I guess it's all the same question, isn't it? And thanks for the compliments, by the way."

"Are you stalling? Because …"

"No. Or yes. I don't know. The answer is complicated. I'm not even sure I know myself." With a knit brow, she contemplated how to respond.

"Is it because of Dad?"

It was, wasn't it. But in what way? "I suppose so." The truth of that response washed over her like wave after wave coming in from the ocean. "Yes. You're right, Noah, but it's not that simple."

"Okay, then explain it to me."

She shifted uncomfortably. He wasn't going to let her off the hook. "It's hard to put it into words. Honestly, I've never thought through it before. But I guess it really is about your dad." She paused to process her own thoughts. Noah waited patiently, not prodding but not turning aside his gaze either.

"You don't make this easy, you know?"

"Just doing my job—you know, being a teenager."

"Okay. I don't think anyone could live up to your dad. He was incredible." She shrugged. "At the same time, what if they *are* like your dad?"

"The positive and negative in the same man."

She nodded. "It would be hard for anyone to match his strengths, and I fear someone might match his faults, faults I never saw until after he died. He even had good traits I wasn't fully aware of until after his death." She smiled ruefully. "It can be scary not knowing the true character of the person in front of you. I think I finally decided it was too much effort to figure it out. It was easier not to try, not to have to."

"That makes sense. I thought maybe it was my fault."

"Your fault? Oh no, not at all."

"Are you sure?"

"Oh, Noah, you were never a problem with any of this. But, to be honest, I probably used you as an excuse to avoid men. I could easily have given you the wrong impression about that. I'm sorry if I did. Forgive me?"

His face relaxed. "Sure. I never heard you say anything like that. I just thought … well, I thought not too many guys would want an instant family or to have to raise someone else's kid." He cast his gaze down.

Brea reached over and lifted his chin. "Noah, do not think for one moment that you made me miss out on anything. You are the best part of my life!"

His eyes met hers at last, scanning for any hint of deception. "Are you sure?" It came out as a mere whisper.

"I'm absolutely sure." She grabbed him in a strong embrace. After a minute, Brea started to laugh.

Noah pulled back and stared at her. "What's funny?"

"Oh, Noah, it actually is your fault I never got serious with anyone."

"What? I thought you were trying to make me feel better."

"I know, but something just dawned on me. Comparing men to your dad was definitely a reason I didn't get serious with anyone, but it wasn't the only one. I wasn't searching for a relationship because my life was already full—because of you! I didn't feel incomplete in any way. If anything, I wanted you to have a dad. But none of the men I met struck me as high enough caliber to be your dad. So, I quit looking."

She threw her head back and laughed. "Noah, you asked me a question I've been avoiding for years. The answer is complicated and multi-layered and yet not. Finally understanding it is a relief."

"I can see that. It wasn't what I was expecting."

"Are you okay with that?"

"Yeah, I think so. It seems fair." But Noah's eyebrows were knit.

Guessing at his concerns, Brea asked, "Do you miss having a dad or wish you had a step-dad?"

"I don't know. It's hard to miss something you don't remember having."

"I wouldn't have thought of it that way, but I understand. You've had to grow up and shoulder a lot for a thirteen-year-old. I'm proud of you."

He shrugged. "I try." But Brea failed to notice that his expression hadn't eased.

Yawning, Noah made his excuses and retreated to bed, exhausted. Brea followed only a moment later, never realizing she'd been both right and wrong. It was definitely complicated, but in more ways than she knew.

ENVELOPE #2

Before they started delving into the family research of who Beniamino might be, sightseeing was their agreed upon focus—when in Rome … and all that. They visited the Pantheon, the Forum, and Colosseum one day. The next was spent at the Vatican, seeing St. Peter's Basilica and the Vatican museums including the Sistine Chapel.

They didn't revisit the serious discussions they'd started, but they did talk, more than they had in months. Every place they went invited a conversation about their favorite parts, the things that most surprised them, and what they wouldn't mind seeing again if they had enough time.

Brea watched Noah's face with fascination. It was soon as easy to read as when he'd been a toddler. Initially, the mask he'd adopted lately still blocked any outward show of emotion, but the more they did together, the less he worked at hiding what he thought.

His face was aglow as he gushed, "Can you believe the Sistine Chapel? I'm glad we borrowed that guy's binoculars, though. We would have missed how detailed it was." And his eyes lit up like a little kid on Christmas at the sight of the Colosseum. "This is so cool, Mom! I had no idea this place was so massive." From one place to the next, Noah and Brea found themselves in awe of places they'd heard about but couldn't possibly have imagined.

But it was the off-the-beaten-path things that seemed to intrigue Noah the most. Brea wasn't surprised that he liked the gladiator school. She even joined him learning how to fight like a gladiator might have. However, she was surprised that he liked visiting the Church of St. Ignatius just as much. It wasn't as well known or as publicized as other sites, but what was interesting about it was its ceiling. It was flat but painted to look like a dome. Noah kept leaning his head back, staring at the wonder above them. Originally painted in 1685 by Andrea Pozzo, the illusion was, in itself, a masterpiece.

When they weren't visiting tourist spots, Noah had them sampling gelatos and bread and pastas and anything with an intriguing Italian name. Normally a picky eater, he was becoming the adventurous one. He didn't like everything they tried, not by a long shot, but he was always polite about it, much to Brea's amazement.

At the end of their first week, they settled down for a rare evening of doing virtually nothing. Having grabbed takeout from the neighborhood restaurant, the two of them settled on their patio to eat and relax.

Between bites, Brea said, "You know, Noah, I'm impressed by you this week. I've seen you try things I never thought you would and with an attitude few thirteen-year-olds exhibit. I don't want this to come out wrong, but how are you doing that?"

"I'm going to take that as a compliment. Honestly, it feels like Mimi gave us this trip. I couldn't honor her memory if I didn't enjoy it to its fullest, could I?"

"No, I guess not. Why do I keep feeling like you're the adult here?"

He gave her a sly smile. "Truth hurts sometimes, doesn't it?"

Brea punched him playfully on the arm. "It appears I need to temper the number of compliments I'm passing out." She tried to look upset, but it wasn't working. "Okay, I admit, you're a good kid."

Instead of seeming pleased, a cloud passed over his face. "Yeah, I'm a real good kid." It came out edged with sarcasm.

"What? You are."

He stopped eating and turned his body to face his mother. "Don't be mad at me, Mom, but I haven't been exactly honest with you lately."

Even though she'd known he'd been hiding things from her, this admission made her stomach drop. With more of a steady voice than she felt, she said, "Okay. What's been going on?"

"It's not as bad as you might think, okay?" When she nodded her understanding, he continued. "Riley invited me to a party. He said it was just a small group so I shouldn't tell you it was a party or anything, you know, in case you got the wrong idea. I shouldn't have listened, but I guess I wanted to believe him." He was no longer meeting his mother's gaze.

Brea didn't turn away, and even though her heart was pounding, she put a comforting hand on top of Noah's, encouraging him to continue. He didn't pull away. "It was bad, Mom." He glanced up at her with shame etched across his face. "His parents were gone and there were a ton of kids there. Alcohol was everywhere. The punch was spiked. I tried some before I realized, but then once I did, I didn't want to look like a jerk, so I had more. I even tried some scotch. The taste of it was nasty at first, but then it kind of warmed me. I liked how it felt. And I didn't feel so shy or awkward. I liked that too.

"I really only took sips for the most part to start with. For whatever reason, I decided that was enough, but I did plan on drinking more later. I know my thinking was all messed up, but I wanted to remember what my first time being drunk felt like, so I decided to spread out my drinking." He shook his head in disgust. "I know that was stupid, but I guess in the end it saved me. I was more clear-headed than everyone else.

"After an hour or so, someone brought out some weed, and I'm pretty sure there were harder drugs in the next room. A kid offered me the weed, but I turned him down. If I'd stuck around much longer, I'm not sure what would have happened. At the time, though, I was happy enough to sit in a corner and watch people. Buzzed as I was, I could still tell they were acting crazy. It was funny until I realized how stupid they were. One kid was playing with a lighter to see if he could burn the hair off his arm without setting his arm on fire. Another girl was dancing and taking her clothes off. Everyone else was either passed out or acting ridiculous.

"Riley came over and offered me something more to drink but I brushed him off. I think I said something like my mom would kill me if she found out. He said, 'Hey, it's easier to get forgiveness than permission. Besides, she'll never even find out.' And all that made me think of Dad. He did things he thought you would never find out about, and you didn't for a while. But when you did, it was so much worse. I couldn't do that to you."

He stopped talking even though it was clear he wasn't done with his confession. Brea thought of Martha's example and waited until he was ready to continue. "When Riley wasn't looking, I took off. It would have been braver of me to stand up to him, but I couldn't do it. I thought the alcohol might give me more courage, but …" He shrugged. "I don't think drinking was helping anyone do the right thing. So, I just slunk out. I didn't want to go home because I figured you'd be able to tell I'd been drinking, even if it wasn't much."

He winced at the memory. "I ended up outside the library. It was closed, but I didn't care. I had my backpack since I'd told you I was going to Riley's to do homework. I pulled out my notebook and started doodling in it. Once my head began to clear, I thought about what Riley said. No one knows more than me that 'It's easier to get forgiveness than permission,' is one of the dumbest things you can say. It's messed up. Look where that got Dad. He's dead, which sucks for him and it sucks for us. So, I made up a new saying and wrote it in my notebook. It says, 'It's easier not to be stupid than to have to fix stupid.' Then later I added, 'but better to fix stupid if you're already there.'" He smiled shyly for the first time since he'd begun.

Brea opened her mouth to speak when Noah put his hand gently on her lips. "Mom, I opened the second envelope. The note inside said: *Share something you've written.* I couldn't share what I'd written without telling you the whole story."

"I'm glad you told me, Noah." She said it softly. Then being careful not to sound harsh or judgmental, she added, "I would have come and gotten you. You could have called me. I would have come."

The harsh tone of his response surprised her. "No. I'm all you've got. You even told me that yourself. I can't mess up."

"Noah, that's not true. We all make mistakes."

"No. You don't understand." He threw his hands up in frustration then retreated into the house without finishing his dinner.

Brea was left to contemplate his confession and his reaction. She'd been so worried about what he'd been hiding, that now he'd told her, she was surprised at how hollow she felt even while feeling relieved. The indiscretion itself was minor given his choice to walk away. Yet their relationship wasn't suddenly better. She hadn't really expected it to be, but a part of her naively hoped it would. Sitting alone, she wondered how to find her way back to her little boy—or find a pathway to get to know the growing young man he was becoming.

With no clear answers, she gathered up the leftovers. Once back inside, she spotted Martha's box where it had found a permanent place on the coffee table. *Share something you've written.* What else had Noah written? She didn't know he'd been writing anything but clearly Martha had. "I didn't even ask about his other writing," she mumbled to herself. Then shaking her head ruefully, she said, "As if I had the chance."

THE BLUE NOTEBOOK

The next morning Noah was up and about early, whistling cheerfully. Brea was pleased with the change in his demeanor but wasn't sure what to make of it. She was hesitant to prod him for an explanation, afraid it might sour his mood.

Before leaving for sightseeing, Brea passed by the coffee table and Martha's box. The lid of the box was off to the side. Envelopes #1 and #2 lay beside it. The third envelope sat on top inside the box. *Brea* was clearly written on it. Her reluctance surprised her. She now understood why Noah had waited. How uncomfortable would following the instructions inside be? What would it cost her this time? She may trust Martha, even know Martha would clearly have their best interests at heart, but it didn't mean what lay inside that envelope would be easy. She turned aside instead, hustling Noah out the door where she didn't have to contemplate her cowardice.

They opted for places to visit that day that didn't need an entrance ticket, such as the Trevi Fountain and the Spanish Steps. Then they took a cab to Trastevere, a neighborhood known for its shops and restaurants.

Brea started the day regretting the fact she hadn't asked Noah about his writing. What did he write about? How much had he written? Was the adage he'd come up with his first, or had he been writing for a while now?

She wanted to know but feared the moment to ask had passed. She should have said something last night, but when she replayed that scene in her head, she couldn't identify a moment when she could have actually brought it up. Things had gone south so quickly and after a seemingly safe topic of conversation.

Maybe the moment hadn't passed yet, but surely opening envelope #3 would signal that she had gone on, that the particular chapter associated with envelope #2 was closed. It was the excuse she kept telling herself to make her feel better about her hesitation.

"Mom, what do you think?" Noah was pointing to a particularly fancy pair of men's tan leather shoes. They had stopped in one of the many shops filled with traditional Italian merchandise. "Do you think they're my style?" He had a twinkle in his eyes.

"Oh, I dare you to wear something like that down the halls of your high school."

"I know. Everyone would be so jealous. I'd never get invited to another party again—you know, because they'd all know they couldn't compete with shoes like those."

Brea smiled, but the mention of parties dampened her spirits. He was a kind and obedient child, but even good kids could get steered in the wrong direction. Noah didn't appear to have noticed her changed demeanor and was browsing through a rack of leather belts.

She thought through what had set him off last night—something about his need to be perfect because he was all she had. Could someone be too good? That didn't seem possible, but maybe in this case it was, in an odd sort of way. It's not that he was too good, it's that he put pressure on himself to be perfect. Even now, he was enjoying this trip, but was it to please Mimi, to please her? Hopefully, underneath all that, he was also enjoying it for himself.

They wandered around Trastevere for the rest of the afternoon. It was so much more than shops and restaurants. The buildings exuded Roman charm.

The church was magnificent without being overwhelming. The small square was picturesque.

Noah selected a restaurant for their dinner that had the right-sized crowd—enough customers to show it made decent food but not so many that they would need to wait for hours before eating. They decided to both try pizza for their entrée. Having peered at the nearby tables, they knew it would be nothing like their pizza back home. By the time it arrived, Brea had decided to ask Noah more about his writing.

"Aren't you going to eat, Mom? This tastes great, but it's different."

He had chosen a red pizza with tomato and mozzarella. Brea ordered a white pizza with mozzarella, peppers, eggplant, and *courgette*, which she learned was zucchini. But food was not on her mind.

"Noah, when we were talking last night … well, I wanted to ask you more about–"

"Yeah, I figured you would. What happened with Riley?"

"I …" She didn't know whether to correct him or just listen to what he had to say. She opted to shut her mouth, nodding for him to continue.

"I know Riley and I used to be best friends, but I didn't like how I felt being at that party. And I really didn't like that he wanted me to lie to you about it. Even worse, I didn't like myself for listening to him."

"So, where do you two stand now? Are you still friends?"

"No. I've barely talked to him since. After telling him I was busy two or three times he got the idea. He walked away from me too. I know that's what I wanted, but it still hurt that he gave up so easily. We were friends for a long time."

"That's tough. So, what now?"

"I've been trying to make new friends, but that's kind of hard, especially at the end of the school year. Most of my other friends are also friends with Riley. They were the other kids at the party, and none of them left like I did. So, that tells you where I stand with them. They didn't exactly reject me, but it's clear I've chosen a different path. We've literally parted ways.

"Mom, to be honest, I wanted to leave before the last few days of school. They're meant to be chill days where you hang out with your friends and sign each other's yearbooks. They would have been pretty lonely ones for me."

"I'm sorry, Noah. I didn't know. I mean, you were always going off to a friend's house … I just assumed. I shouldn't have." She added in a gentle tone, "Where did you go?"

He shrugged. "Mostly to the library. I've become friends with the librarians, so I wasn't completely lying." He gave her a sheepish look.

She smiled. "Fair enough."

"I didn't want you to worry about me having friends, or the wrong kind of friends—like Dad did."

"Oh, Noah, you put way too much pressure on yourself. You don't have to be perfect. Is that why you've stopped talking to me lately—out of guilt, that somehow you weren't perfect so you couldn't face me?"

"Mom, you don't have anyone but me. I can't screw things up, and that's all I was doing. In some ways, I think I wanted to make you mad enough at me that you'd say I was an awful kid. Then I'd be off the hook, and I wouldn't have to worry about getting close to perfect but falling short."

"Noah, I need to tell you something. But before I do, is there any other unseemly behavior that I need to know about? Anything else we need to get cleared up?"

"You want to know all my secrets?"

"No. You can have things that you want to keep private as long as they're not damaging to yourself or others. Are we clear on that?"

"Yes. And, to answer your question, no, there's nothing else you need to worry about."

"Okay. I want you to listen to me very carefully because this is really important. How about we take a break from being perfect and accept that life can be challenging and messy? Can we agree to cut each other some slack?"

"Yeah, I guess so."

"Noah, I was a teenager once. I've always tried to be a decent person, for the most part at least. But I made mistakes. I still make mistakes. As your mom, I would much rather help you through the hard times than be deceived that everything is peachy."

Noah surprised her by grinning. "Can I borrow that?"

"Borrow what?"

"That thing about helping you through the hard times instead of thinking everything is peachy?"

"You lost me, Noah."

"I told you about the saying I made up, about how it's easier not to be stupid than to have to fix stupid. I have a bunch of sayings like that. Some are better than others, but I like what you said. I'd like to add it, if it's okay."

"Of course it's okay. Actually, Noah, that's what I was trying to ask you about earlier. I want to learn more about your writing."

"Oh, I thought you wanted to know about …"

"I know. Should I have stopped you?" She raised her eyebrows to see if she'd made the right call.

"Well, probably not. Once I told you about Riley last night, I wanted to tell you everything. I just needed a way to get started."

"I'm glad you told me. Thanks." She gave him a reassuring smile. "Now, tell me more about what you write."

He flashed a boyish grin. "I just jot things down when I like the way they sound. We had an assignment in English to collect quotes from famous people. I called it my old, dead dudes project, but I ended up liking the idea. So, sometimes I write down things people have said, but now I'm writing down more things I come up with myself, you know, comforting thoughts or rules to live by."

"I like that. Do you write them in your notebook? Oh! Your notebook! You dropped a notebook one day. It was dark blue, and I didn't recognize it. You sort of freaked out when I picked it up. Was that …?"

"Yeah. Sorry about that. I've been pretty protective of it. It's like it's a little piece of my soul or something." He scrunched up his face. "That sounds funny when I say it that way, but I don't know how else to describe it."

"I understand, and I think you put it nicely. For the record, I'd love to hear more of what you've written, but it belongs to you. So, share something with me when and if you want to. It's one of those private things that you get to decide about. Are we clear on that? Again, as long as there's nothing harmful to you or others in what you write."

"Thanks, Mom."

With the honest admissions, their talk took on a lighter tone. They enjoyed the rest of their dinner for the company as much as the pizza, which they found to be delicious.

It was late by the time they returned to their apartment. A cab dropped them off nearby in front of their favorite gelato shop. They ate it while lazily wending their way back home.

Brea's eyes fixed on Martha's box as soon as they entered the apartment, and her heart took a small leap. It wasn't the thought of the third envelope that struck her this time. It was what was written on Noah's note. *Share something you've written.* It hit her again that Martha knew he was writing. She knew at least six months ago, before she died.

It was a comforting thought—Brea trusted Martha, and Noah had had someone to confide in that he also trusted. But that thought also brought the glaring reality that she was not that trusted person. Every mom knows kids keep secrets. Every mom knows there's a whole lot she doesn't know about her child. But his writing was important to him. It was special. It was a positive thing. And she hadn't even known it existed.

ORVIETO

Despite the questions Brea still had about Noah—who he truly was, who he was becoming—the question of who Benjamin Roberts was came up next in their plans. Given their late night, they got up later than they'd wanted, but still were soon on their way to the small hill town of Orvieto, the birthplace of Beniamino.

"I know this is your thing, Mom, but it's still exciting, isn't it? I mean, he's my ancestor too. And we don't know much about him. I can't believe he lived here. That is so cool!"

"Yeah. I didn't think I'd ever care that much about someone who lived over a hundred years ago, but I know what you mean. I want to know about his life. I want to walk where he walked. I can't explain it."

They both eagerly watched out the train window as the countryside passed by with its olive groves and hinted-at cities off in the distance. In under two hours, they arrived at the Orvieto station.

Hopping off the train with their day packs, they made their way to the funicular, a cable railroad that would take them from the new town of Orvieto to the old town on top of the hill. The tracks went up the side of the mountain, having been cut directly into the rock. At one point, it ducked through a small tunnel.

"I googled it, Mom. This was built in 1990, but the original funicular here was built in 1888."

"That means Beniamino …"

"Yep. He was born in 1895. He would have ridden up and down the mountain on this."

They grew silent, enjoying their ascent with a new perspective. Before long, they arrived at the Piazza Cahen in the city center.

Their first stop, as planned, was the City Office of Orvieto, basically the town hall archives. With the help of their phrase book and online translating tools, they managed to get their request across to the somewhat bewildered town clerk. *Antenato*, which is Italian for a male ancestor, was the word that made her eyes open wide. She then ushered them back into a room where they could go through old records.

A daunting collection of church records greeted them. Several parishes existed in Orvieto, but the city had collected their records, at least for the time frame they were researching. Thankfully, the town clerk found someone to help them navigate the old volumes. Their helper, they learned, was named Dino, and he spoke slightly more English than the clerk.

"*Antenato*," they kept repeating, along with "Orvieto." Brea wrote the date 23-2-1895 on a piece of paper to show him, remembering to put the day before the month. Dino nodded and soon located a series of books for them to sort through. When it came to the name they were searching for, it got a little more complicated. "Beniamino" followed by a shrug didn't seem to convey its meaning.

Noah finally had an idea. He wrote "Beniamino ______" and drew a crude boot-shaped outline of Italy. He then drew an arrow, a somewhat-distinguishable outline of the United States, and the name "Benjamin Roberts." Pointing to himself and his mother, he said, "*Antenato*." As an extra touch, he added 1895 under Beniamino in Italy and 1919 under Benjamin Roberts in the United States.

"Aaah," Dino said, nodding. Through a series of gestures, he mimicked the concept of Beniamino being a baby in Orvieto, growing up, and traveling by boat to the U.S. where he became Benjamin.

With this joint understanding came a shared sense of purpose. All three of them selected a book of records to scour. They were hoping to find a Beniamino with a surname that started with "R" who was born in 1895. If he picked a name like Benjamin which was close to Beniamino, it made sense that his last name would be similar to Roberts. That was at least the hope.

About an hour into their search, Noah let out an excited yell. "I think I found him! I think this is the right guy!" Brea jumped up, almost upsetting the book on her lap. Dino responded nearly as quickly. He may not have understood Noah's words, but he understood the excitement in his voice.

"Where? Show me."

"Right here, Mom." Noah pointed to a line in the parish record. "It's hard to read the cursive handwriting, but the birthdate is 23-2, and this whole page is 1895. I think that says Beniamino."

Dino leaned over and read, "Beniamino Robustelli." He looked up at the two of them and beamed. "*Il tuo antenato*," he said, pointing to the two of them—your ancestor.

"Yes, our ancestor," Brea repeated. She was surprised to find tears pooling in her eyes. Gaining her composure, she pulled paper and pencil out of her purse. Noah took a picture of the record with his phone, after verifying such a thing was okay with Dino, while Brea copied down the name of Beniamino's parents, Liberto and Stefania Robustelli. Other than those names and his birthdate, nothing else was written.

In an effort to be thorough, they spent another hour culling through records to make sure they had found the right Beniamino. They came across other baby boys born on that same date, and they found other Beniamino's, but no other listing connecting both of them together. "We really found him," Brea whispered to herself when they finally exhausted the other possibilities.

Noah, having overheard her, carefully returned the book he'd finished examining to its rightful place then sat down next to his mother. "Yeah, we did it." He put his head on her shoulder like he used to do when he was little.

"*Mi scusi*," Dino said. "*Fotografia*." He gestured to borrow one of their phones. Brea handed hers over, and Dino took several pictures of the two of them sitting serenely side by side.

When he returned her phone, he said, "*Orvieto. Terni provincia. Umbria regione.*" She nodded her understanding. He wrote the three names down for her. He then said, "*Record militare,*" which was easy enough to understand, while pointing to Terni.

"We can find his military record in the Terni province?" Brea said.

Dino nodded. "But first, enjoy Orvieto," he said in heavily accented English with a broad grin.

"We will," Noah said.

Enjoy Orvieto they did. Dino directed them to a bike rental. "For exploring," he said. Then before he left them, Dino made sure to point out the Church of Sant'Andrea, the source of Beniamino Robustelli's birth record.

Orvieto was home to a number of churches. They parked their bikes and explored a few of them, especially the Church of Sant'Andrea. They found the Duomo di Orvieto to be quite stunning, but it didn't elicit the same familial connection that Beniamino's church had.

After exploring other monuments and museums, they returned their bikes and joined a tour of Orvieto's Underground. Carved into the rock underneath the city was an extensive array of grottoes, over 1200 of them, built by the Etruscans five hundred years before Christ. Even though they existed for centuries before Beniamino was born, they had been lost to some extent to the knowledge of the people who lived above them. One large room shown to them had served as a bomb shelter for the residents of Orvieto during World War II.

"Do you think Beniamino's family knew about these?" Noah whispered to his mom.

"I don't know, but I was wondering the same thing."

They were learning bits and pieces about Beniamino, but he had parents and ancestors, *antenati* (the plural of *antenato*, Brea learned), of his own, which made them theirs too. This might turn into the first trip of many. There was so much to learn and discover.

Exhausted but happy from their productive day, Brea and Noah dragged themselves back to their home away from home in Rome. Brea had no idea what Noah did, but she fell asleep in her clothes on top of her covers.

THE BROTHERS

Even before Dino suggested it, Brea had considered Terni to be a possible stop on their itinerary. It both surpassed their expectations and left them disappointed.

Like with Orvieto, they started by searching for more information about Beniamino Robustelli with plans to sightsee afterwards. Finding themselves in a records office again, they asked about the military records for their *antenato*.

This clerk, a middle-aged Italian woman, spoke excellent English. "What time frame are you interested in?"

"World War I. He would have fought before immigrating to the United States in 1919."

"I'm sorry, but we don't have those records."

"You don't? Why not?"

"Terni province was created in 1927. We are part of Umbria but didn't exist as such until well after World War I."

"Oh," Noah sighed. "Where would we find his records then?"

"You'll need to go to Perugia, the regional capital of Umbria. You should be able to find everything you need there."

"Where is Perugia?"

"It's about an hour or so north of here."

Crestfallen, both Noah and Brea collapsed into nearby chairs. Of course, it couldn't be as easy as they'd hoped.

Noticing their reaction, the clerk continued with a bright voice. "But when you do find the records, they should be very helpful. Military service was compulsory for every male until 2005. Conscription of all males at the age of 18 began in 1865, and the records that are kept are meticulous. They list birthdate, birthplace, age, residence, occupation, a physical description, family members, and all about the location and nature of their service. It will be well worth your trip."

"Thank you. I know it will," Brea said, trying to sound grateful.

"Well," Noah said, squeezing out a smile, "since we're here, let's make the most of it." Turning to the clerk, he asked, "What are the best things to do in Terni?"

The clerk's face brightened. "You'll want to see the old Roman amphitheater. It's no Colosseum, but it's still quite impressive. Then take lunch with you and head out to the Black River Park. You can hike and bike all over it. It's really beautiful. But the best part is the Marmore Falls. They're impressive, but even more so when you realize they're man-made. The Romans created them in antiquity. I promise, you've never seen anything like them."

Despite their initial disappointment, the clerk had been right about everything. Terni was a place they were glad not to have missed. After visiting the amphitheater, they hiked, snacked, hiked some more, and took pictures— selfies, scenery, selfies in front of scenery, and an occasional accidental picture of a finger or the inside of a pocket. The best part to Brea was the non-stop talking they did, when they weren't out of breath from an arduous incline.

At the end of another exhausting day, they made their way one last time back to Rome. After one more day to sightsee or shop in Rome, they would be heading north to Florence—with a stop off in the town of Perugia.

. . .

The next day came with mixed emotions. They had seen everything on their list in Rome, and the thought of going on to a new city with new things to do and see was exciting. But Rome felt comfortable. Coming back to the same place after sightseeing or taking day trips to Orvieto and Terni was relaxing. They would be sad to leave it behind.

As a last hurrah, they decided to pay for a tour from the back of a Vespa. Their two guides turned out to be brothers Carlo and Matteo, young men with dimples in their chins and matching curly brown hair and winning smiles. They asked what Brea and Noah wanted to see. Glancing at each other, they laughed in unison, and said, "Surprise us."

It took a few minutes to sort out exactly what they meant by that. So, Brea and Noah listed all the places they'd been, highlighting their favorites. But in the end, Brea summed it up with, "Show us Rome the way you see it. Show us what you love about the city, the things we might not normally see."

The result was a memorable day. Their guides/drivers took them to two different locations—Gianicolo Hill and the Orange Gardens on Aventine Hill—where they caught breathtaking, panoramic views of Rome. The brothers took Brea and Noah to their favorite, out-of-the way restaurant for lunch, helping them order the best dishes, most of them off menu. Then they capped off the afternoon visiting several small shops filled with items made by local artisans.

After the shopping, the guides collected their pay but surprised the mother-son pair with one last suggestion. "We have enjoyed the day as much as you have. It's not often we get to take guests to see anything other than the most popular sites. This has been a refreshing change of pace," Carlo said. "So, would you join us for a family dinner? Matteo called our mother. She is already cooking up everything in the house in the hopes you will come. No pressure, but she will probably die of heartbreak if you do not accept."

Matteo then pulled out his phone and showed them a picture of a table laden with food. "This was our dinner on Sunday. Our *mamma*, our mother, apologized for not making enough food because she'd been under the weather. But, be warned, she's feeling better now."

Noah's eyes grew wide. The answer was obvious if it was up to him. He peered expectantly at his mom. Brea didn't hesitate. "We would love to come. *Grazie.*"

Matteo and Carlo's mother met every preconceived notion Brea and Noah had of an Italian mother or grandmother. She was warm, inviting, and spoke effusively to them in Italian as if they understood every word. And in many ways, they did. Between the kisses on both cheeks, the arms thrown into the air, and the broad grin, it was hard to misunderstand her intent. Her name was Carina. However, as both sons attested, she preferred they call her *Mamma*, which was not hard to do.

While they enjoyed their delicious appetizers, Matteo introduced them around the table. Seated next to *Mamma* was a small, ancient-looking woman—*Mamma's mamma, Nonna* or Grandma. Next to *Nonna* was their aunt and uncle, Zia Isabella and Zio Dante. An older man named Aldo was next, although despite comparing notes later, Brea and Noah couldn't piece together how he was related. After Aldo came several cousins whose names got lost in the hubbub of food, the passing of food, and multiple loud conversations going on around them.

Over the course of the long, delicious dinner, they learned from Carlo that their *padre,* or father, died when they were young. Their *mamma* had worked hard cooking and cleaning for others to provide for them. But now, with their Vespa guided tours, they were taking care of her.

"Really?" Noah said. "My dad died too." He seemed to bask in the connection.

Matteo and Carlo both perked up. "Ah. That explains why you were so protective of your mother all day," Matteo said.

"Protective?"

"Yes. When you met us, you stood between your mother and the two of us," Matteo said.

"I did?"

"You did," Carlo said, "And when we took you to overlook the city, you ran ahead to make sure it was safe before coming back to walk beside your mother."

"I didn't realize I did that. How come no one's ever pointed that out before?"

"Maybe they just didn't say anything, or more likely, they didn't notice. Carlo and I have been protective of our mother for a long time. You remind us of ourselves."

"That's cool. Did you guys know you were doing that?" Noah said.

"Not at first, but after a while we began to see it in each other. We started fighting over who was taking better care of our *mamma*. Once we had enough sense to stop arguing about it, we made a pact that we would always watch over her. That's why we went into business together."

Matteo chuckled, "It's also probably the reason we're not married. We don't have time for anyone else."

"Although that will probably change. *Mamma* has started hinting she wants *nipoti*, grandchildren, before she gets too old to enjoy them."

Brea, who was finding her seat between Carlo and Noah to be an intrusion, said, "I can tell you two love your mother very much. Noah has always been a great son too." She smiled at him but resisted the urge to ruffle his hair. "And now, would you mind if I traded places?"

After swapping seats with Carlo so that Noah had a brother on either side of him, Brea heard him ask, "Were you ever mad that your dad was dead, that you have to be the ones taking care of your mom?" She grinned as the three of them talked non-stop the rest of the meal while still somehow succeeding in clearing their plates multiple times.

Brea did her best to hold her own with the other family members and dinner guests. None of them spoke English, so they managed with lots of gestures and smiles. Brea made an attempt to learn the Italian words for various things—*pane* was bread, *frutta* meant fruit, *tavolo* for table, *famiglia* meant family, and so on, some more obvious than others. The mention of family prompted the sharing of photographs from their phones. Brea saw many pictures of interesting people with no idea who any of them were, yet they somehow felt like life-long friends—both the people pictured and those around the table.

With reluctance they finally parted to return to their apartment, a place that had felt so much like a home away from home that now felt empty and lonely. Noah's face was still aglow, however. "Mom, Carlo and Matteo gave me their address and their email. They want me to write them and stay in touch. If we come back, we have to visit them again."

"Well, I'm thinking we're going to have to come back anyway. I mean, this is our long-lost homeland, right?"

"Yeah. You're right!"

So much of their trip was still ahead of them, but already, it had been well worth it.

SERVICE RECORDS

Brea and Noah's next day started before the sun. They caught an early train to Perugia, situated one hundred miles north of Rome. After spending the day tracking down Beniamino's civil service records, they planned to hop back on the train for the two-hour trip to Florence.

They struggled to find the building that housed the military records they were seeking, but once they were in the right place, everything else was surprisingly easy. The records were all digitized, and even though they were in Italian, they were easy to search.

Beniamino Robustelli began his three premilitary years in 1913 when he turned 18. The *Liste de Leva*, or conscription record, was wonderfully detailed. Along with his birthdate, it listed his parent's names, the same Liberto and Stefania Robustelli from his birth record; his place of residence, still Orvieto; his height, 5' 10"; and that he had dark brown hair, brown eyes, and was single.

The attendant in the records' office, Lauretta, showed them how to find the *Liste d'Estrazione*, the draft record, for Beniamino Robustelli. He was drafted at the age of 21 in 1916. This record included much of the previous information along with the results of a physical exam. He was deemed physically, mentally, and legally eligible to serve in the Italian army.

The most interesting addition to this record was his listed occupation. Beniamino was a teacher, a language teacher. It appeared from the notes that he spoke French in addition to his native Italian.

When Lauretta broke for lunch, she gave them recommendations of places they might like to eat, promising to return in an hour and a half to help them finish their search. Reluctant as they were to stop in the middle of things, their small, early breakfast left them more than willing to take a lunch break.

Right on time an hour and a half later, Lauretta met them outside the records office, unlocked it, and ushered them back inside. "You will want to check two more records—*Registro di Ruolo* and *Foglio di Congedo Illimitato*. They are the service and discharge records."

Those last two contained a lot of information, all in Italian. Lauretta helped them print out copies for them to keep. Then she painstakingly walked them through the English translation of what they had.

"His service record is a list of where he served and when, without much explanation. But, here, this is interesting. He became a personal assistant and messenger for General Colombo." She pointed to the part of the record she was referring to. "It mentions his language skills, but other than that, there isn't much information. It appears that what he did was censored or secret. Sorry there isn't more about his service.

"It does say he was wounded while on an errand or a mission for the General. He ended up with wounds in his leg and head. Wherever he was, it seems he was brought back to the U.S. Army Base Hospital in Vicenza."

"Vicenza? Noah, that's what his record from Ellis Island said. His last place of residence was Vicenza, remember?"

"I'd forgotten that. Does the record say anything else?"

Lauretta scanned the papers. "He never returned to active duty after that and was discharged in November 1918."

"Was that because the war ended?" Brea asked.

"It could be that or because of his wounds. I can't tell for sure."

"Where is Vicenza?" Noah asked. "Is there anything there anymore?"

"It's west of Venice, maybe an hour away. But I have no idea if any information is there. World War I was a long time ago."

"Thank you, Lauretta. You've been very helpful," Brea said as they gathered up their copies of the records.

It was still early afternoon. With Lauretta's help, they'd finished quickly. "Noah, what do you want to do? We could head to Florence right now. That would give us time to get settled and have a nice dinner."

"Or …?"

"Or, we could see what Perugia has to offer."

"Why don't we wander around a bit. We might as well while we're here. But I don't want to take too long. I'd still like to get to Florence before it's too late."

"Sounds like a plan."

Brea popped her head back into the records office. "Lauretta, if you only had a couple hours to spend in Perugia, what would you do?"

Lauretta laughed. "I don't know that I'm the person to ask. I love all the old buildings and churches, but I'd go to the chocolate factory myself. I think it's hard to beat chocolate."

Noah, standing nearby, said, "I agree with her!"

The balance they struck was peering at the old buildings on their way to the Perugina Chocolate Factory just outside the city center. They smelled the factory long before they arrived which reinforced their choice.

If they'd planned ahead, they learned they could have joined a chocolate-making class instead of simply a tour. "That would have been fun," Noah said, "but as long as we stop in the gift shop, I'm fine with the tour."

An hour later, loaded down with more chocolate than two people should eat in a week, they made their way back to the train station. After retrieving their luggage from a locker, they boarded a train for the two-hour ride to Florence. They would arrive in time to get settled and have a late dinner. Both of them dozed along the way—in between snacking on chocolate.

. . .

Florence was like the other Italian cities they had visited and not like them at all. "It feels the same in some ways, maybe because everyone is speaking a language I can't understand," Noah said upon arrival. "Even the red roofs and buildings look similar, but somehow it's just different."

"I know what you mean. I think it's like visiting two American cities. They share so much yet still have their own unique personalities."

"I guess that's it. I got used to seeing the Colosseum in Rome, and Orvieto was all about being on top of that hill. Compared to Rome, Florence is definitely smaller."

"Yeah. I like that about it. So far, anyway. I wonder how different the food will be."

Once they dropped off their bags in their rented apartment, they had a chance to find out about the food. Their host had suggested a restaurant around the corner, which they were eager to try.

They recognized a few items on the menu, but most were new. "I'm guessing something with Florentine in the name is a specialty of Florence."

"That seems obvious, doesn't it?" Noah rolled his eyes.

"Thanks, kiddo. I appreciate your confidence in my powers of observation. What are you going to try? I want to order something different."

In the end, they tried a seafood stew and a pasta dish. The variety of seafood proved to be a bit much for Noah's taste buds, but they both loved the pasta. And even though they were full, they both ordered a serving of sorbet—one lemon and the other raspberry.

As they walked back to their flat after dinner, Noah said, "That's better sorbet than we get at home. And the gelato we've eaten in Italy is a ton better than any I've tasted before. I could get used to this."

"Agreed. But I think my favorite food, outside of desserts, would have to be the food at Matteo and Carlo's home. It was delicious, but it probably has more to do with the atmosphere than the food itself. It was like having family gathered for a big Thanksgiving dinner."

"Yeah. I hadn't thought about it that way. It felt like comfort food to me, but I didn't know why I felt that way. It's not like it was food I'd eaten before. But, you're right, I can't think about the food without thinking of Matteo and Carlo and how friendly they were."

"Yes, they were. You'll have to make sure and email them."

Noah grinned. "I already did. I emailed them while we were on the train."

"That's great."

"Thanks. And Carlo emailed me back—while we were eating dinner."

"Ahh, that explains the phone thing when we were eating."

Noah chuckled. "I know, I know. We try to avoid being on our phones during dinner. Do you forgive me?"

"Of course I do." Brea smiled to herself. Forgiving him for something so little was easy—especially when they were talking to each other again. He wasn't her little boy anymore, and she knew he never would be again, but this teenage version was shaping up to be one amazing kid.

LEANING

They spent the next few days exploring all that Florence had to offer, which could be summed up as art and architecture in all its various forms. Brea enjoyed watching Noah as much as seeing the famous art she'd heard about her whole life. He was fascinated by the little details of the art, like how a marble statue could look like a soft, gently draped fabric, or how a carved or painted hand contained so many realistic elements. He didn't care for the saints painted with golden halos and pasted beatific smiles, but he loved the dogs and cats milling around their feet.

"Mom, we should get a dog. How come we never thought of getting a dog?" he said while staring at a small pup in the corner of a very large painting.

"I … I don't know. That sounds like a great idea. We'll have to explore that when we get home."

Brea was still lost in thought about getting a puppy when Noah moved onto the next thing. "Why are some of the baby Jesus' round and fat and other paintings make him look like an old man?"

"It depends on the style of the time and how the artist chose to depict the people he painted. I know in one period of art history, people wanted Jesus, even as a baby, to be the man he became. So, they painted his face to appear that way. But there's a lot more I don't know about it. I'm sure we can pick up an art history book in the gift shop that can explain it better than that, if you're interested."

"Yeah. I think that would be cool." And then he was on to the next thing.

. . .

On their last day in Florence, they opted to spend most of it taking a day trip to Pisa. Under an hour away by high-speed train, they found it well worth their time, even though the only thing of real interest to them was the Leaning Tower of Pisa.

Taking a chance, they stopped at the ticket office first to see if there were any time slots available to climb to the top of the tower. "You are lucky. I have room for two at 14:15. Most days we are full up. If you were here a month later, you would have no chance of getting in without booking ahead of time."

"We'll take them. Thank you. *Grazie.*"

"I thought we were going to have to settle for taking the obligatory photo where we're holding up the tower," Noah said. "So, this is turning out great."

"Yes," Brea said without enthusiasm. She was staring up at the marble edifice tilting its mass over them. If it hadn't fallen over in 800 years, it wasn't likely to now, right? Still, she wasn't as grateful as Noah was that they'd been able to get tickets. If a child under 18 hadn't required the accompaniment of an adult, she would have been content to let him climb it on his own. *Do something Noah wants to do that you don't.* Why did Martha's words have to keep coming back to her? She quickly buried that thought because the next thought was a reminder that she had yet to open envelope #3.

"Well, why don't we take those pictures. You first."

Noah grimaced while "straining" to keep the tower from falling over. When Brea had done the same, they compared photos. The resulting images made them both snicker and cringe.

"Those are ridiculous. And I love them!" Brea said. Then she quickly texted them to both sets of grandparents.

Surprising to both of them, they found plenty to keep them busy until it was time to climb the tower. The neighboring baptistery and cathedral were large and impressive. Even the old cemetery in the square was beautiful and sublime. Finally, they grabbed some food and nibbled it while waiting for their time slot to arrive.

Climbing the tilting building up the narrow interior staircase was a bit disconcerting to Brea, but Noah loved every minute of it. "This is so cool, Mom!"

They paused at several windows along the way to peer out below them, each time the ground growing farther and farther away. "It's good I don't have a fear of heights or get claustrophobic," Brea said as a group going down squeezed past them on their way up.

Noah just laughed. "If you can raise a kid on your own, you can handle the Leaning Tower of Pisa."

Brea couldn't argue with that, and by the time they reached the top, she was as excited as Noah was to see the view over the city. It was breathtaking. They walked all around the top to see what was visible in every direction.

"Honestly, Noah, I wasn't so sure I wanted to come up here. But I'm glad I did. This is incredible!"

"Yeah, stick with me. I won't steer you wrong."

Brea gave him an exaggerated eye roll, but she didn't have any comeback.

After their descent, they grabbed a gelato and took an unhurried stroll along the Arno River. "This is nice, Mom. I thought a walk along the river would be boring. I figured agreeing to this was payback for your willingness to climb the tower, but, it's not bad. It's peaceful here."

"Yeah, stick with me. I won't steer you wrong."

Noah laughed. "I guess I deserved that."

When their gelatos were finished, they turned down a nearby lane and made their way through the narrow medieval streets. Stores of all kinds surrounded them. They ventured into the more intriguing ones.

While they found many interesting items, they only bought a few. The reality of needing to haul around all their purchases sank in when they left Rome more laden down than they had anticipated.

. . .

They made it back to Florence in time for an early dinner by European standards. Even with the more relaxed pace of Italy, they found themselves back at their flat with time left in their evening. Noah disappeared into his computer while Brea pored over their plans for the following few days.

Venice was next on their agenda, but Brea was managing to squeeze in a trip to Vicenza. They might not find any more about Beniamino, but she couldn't come this close and not try. So far, they had added only a few facts and dates to their knowledge about him, but it was enough for him to become real in her head. He felt like a friend in addition to a great-grandfather.

Surprised she hadn't thought of it sooner, she texted her dad. "Do you have any photographs of your grandfather? I want to know what Beniamino looked like. He isn't just a dead ancestor to me anymore. I'd like to be able to picture his face."

Her dad responded quickly. "Don't know. I'll look."

Brea was setting her phone back down when Noah approached. "Mom, can we go to Germany? There's a really cool castle, Neuschwanstein Castle. I bet you'd like it. It's not that far into Germany."

"Yeah, I've heard of it. It's the model for the Disneyland castle, I think. I'd love to see it. I'm just surprised you do."

"Well, there *is* this awesome luge run nearby. You ride along a steel track down a mountain on your own sled." He had a guilty twinkle. "It sounds really fun, Mom."

"Oh, I see how it is."

Noah shrugged but was still smiling.

"Oh sure, why not? Let's see what we can figure out. I mean we already fit in Perugia, and we're going to add Vicenza. Why not add Germany? We've come this far."

"Thanks, Mom."

"Is that what you've been busy with on your computer? You've seemed rather absorbed."

"A little. Mostly I'm trying to find more about George Harrison and Viborgne."

"Are you learning anything?"

"Nothing more about George, but I'm finding bits of info about Viborgne. It's a small town, which I already knew, but I was trying to connect it to World War I. The problem is when you google Viborgne and World War I, you often come up with World War II information instead. I have to admit at first that was frustrating. But I finally decided to read some of those articles to see if I could learn anything about Viborgne."

"Did that help?"

"Not to start with. But then I found an interesting one. It talked about the church in Viborgne. It's in the center of town, and the article said it lost its steeple in World War II. I thought about our research for Beniamino and realized the church might be a place to find information. I haven't found any online records for the people in Viborgne, but if the church wasn't damaged any more than its steeple, maybe they have records in their archives. Or maybe there are city records in a town hall. The article didn't say if any other part of the church was destroyed, but it did mention that the steeple had also been damaged in World War I."

"Oh, that's interesting."

"I know. It's not much to go on yet, but it does tie Viborgne to World War I, which is more than I'd come up with before. And it tells us the church has been around that long, although that's not a surprise."

"No, not really. I'm constantly amazed by how old things are here. Well, what you learned is a start."

"Yep. Good night, Mom. Thanks for the Germany thing. You won't regret it."

"I hope not." Noah turned to leave, when Brea called him back. "Hey, did you say how fast those sleds get going down the mountain?"

He grinned. "Nope, I didn't."

VICENZA

Checkout was at 11:00, and Brea intended to let Noah sleep until 10:00. That would give him time to pack his things and grab some breakfast. So, she was surprised coming out of her bedroom at 9:15 to find Noah sitting at the kitchen table with his laptop open in front of him. He seemed lost in thought so she didn't disturb him. Walking past, she could see he was trying to learn more about Viborgne. She also noticed his writing notebook was open facedown next to him. He was writing more. The thought made her smile.

Instead of needing to wake him, she had to rouse him from his research at 10:00. "Hey, Noah, we need to get going. We've got to check out then catch the train for Venice."

"Oh, right. Be ready in a sec."

Before long they were headed to Venice on a high-speed train. It only took two hours that way, and they arrived with time left in the day.

"Hey, Mom, can we take a gondola ride? That sounds so cool." They were wending their way through the city to their vacation rental.

"Sure, if you want. But I was thinking instead you might like taking rowing lessons and learn how to be your own gondolier," Brea said with a grin.

"Really? You can do that? Cool."

"You're not the only one doing a little internet research this morning. I booked us lessons for tomorrow morning, with an option to cancel this afternoon if you weren't on board with the idea. Although I figured that was highly unlikely."

"That sounds awesome!"

"Well, if you like that, I'm guessing you're going to love where we're staying."

Brea was right. Their vacation rental was a two-bedroom apartment with a living room window that opened right onto a canal. Noah dumped his bag, threw open the window, and leaned out. Being on the second floor, they were above the water but not by much.

"Oh, cool!"

Brea joined him at the window. "Yeah, wow."

"Let's go check it out."

A short distance from the front door of their building, a small alleyway led to the edge of the water. If they glanced to the left, they could see where this canal connected to the Grand Canal a short distance away.

Brea smiled and shivered at the same time. "This is amazing, but if I lived here, I'd be worried about flooding."

"That's because you're a mom. And I read that they have floods all the time. So…," Noah shrugged, "I guess you get used to it."

"That's a weird thing to have to get used to."

"Probably, but it would be worth it." He spun around to explore where the alley led in the other direction. Brea had no choice but to follow.

By the time they returned that night, their feet were sore but their spirits were high. They'd been to Piazzo San Marco or St Mark's Square, visited a number of quaint shops, and sampled a variety of street food—most of which they enjoyed. The next day promised to be just as interesting, and they fell into their beds expectant yet exhausted.

. . .

The next day did not disappoint. Excited but slightly nervous, Noah and Brea made their way to the canal where they would have their rowing lessons. Their instructor, Elisa, introduced herself then helped them climb into the *batela a code di gambero*, a traditional "shrimp-tailed" boat. Shorter than a gondola, but wider by comparison, the *batela* was a stable craft, perfect for learning. Rowing Venetian style was different than they expected and not at all intuitive. At first, they practiced rowing standing up inside the prow. Once they felt comfortable with that, Elisa gave them the option of going out into the lagoon where they could try rowing standing on the stern, no longer tucked safely inside the *batela* itself. Noah, much to his delight, mastered standing up while finding the right cadence of pushing forward more easily than Brea did. Elisa praised Noah for being a quick learner and told Brea, "Keep trying. You'll get better." Eventually, and with a little determination, she managed an adequate job.

"Not bad, Mom. You're a good sport," Noah said while suppressing a grin.

"Thanks, but could you try looking a little less smug?"

After their lessons, Brea was relieved to be back on solid ground. They took their time to wander through the city, taking in the sights of Venice, visiting the Doge's Palace and the famous Bridge of Sighs, crossing the Grand Canal on the Rialto Bridge, then spending time in the nearby market.

All too soon, their day was over. They had plans to visit Vicenza the next day. Depending on how long they spent there, they might have more time to explore Venice, which had entranced them.

Before climbing into bed, Brea said, "Noah, we have a slim chance of learning anything about Beniamino in Vicenza. Are you sure you don't mind taking the time to go?"

"No. It's kind of interesting, actually. And it's real."

"Real?"

"Yeah, it's not like a movie or a book where everything is tied up in a neat, little package, where every clue leads to a discovery. I'm curious if we'll find anything there." He shrugged. "Besides, it's interesting to see how all the Italian towns we've visited are alike and how they're different. You know, like people. People are people anywhere you go. We have so much in common, but we're unique too."

Brea stopped walking to study her son. "That's quite insightful. Have you written that in your notebook?"

Noah beamed. "Not yet, but I think I'll add it."

. . .

Vicenza, directly west of Venice, was about an hour away by train. Their heads turned every which way as they made their way from the train station to the center of town where the town hall was conveniently located.

Brea and Noah knew they weren't trying to find the typical birth certificate or church record. After being passed from one non-English speaking person to another, they finally landed in the office of Flavio Bianchi. After a phone call, his nephew, Brando, joined them. Mr. Bianchi was the city historian and Brando spoke decent English. With a fair amount of back and forth, they were able to piece together the story they were interested in.

As they understood it, the U.S. Army Base Hospital No. 102 was the former Rossi Industrial School. It was quickly turned into a hospital and started accepting patients in September 1918 not long before the end of the war. Situated just fifteen miles from the Italian front, the hospital took in both Italian and American soldiers and treated wounds and illnesses, such as the Spanish Influenza. Set up by a doctor from Loyola University Medical School, it was referred to as the Loyola Unit and was staffed with U.S. Army doctors and nurses along with nurses from the Daughters of Charity.

Brea had brought the printouts of Beniamino's military records with her. She pulled out his service record and showed it to Mr. Bianchi and his nephew.

They conferred together, pointing out various dates and entries. "Yes," Brando finally said, "He was injured and eventually sent to the U.S. Army Base Hospital No. 102 in September 1918. The hospital was open only a few months, but he was here almost that whole time. He was discharged as they started shutting things down."

His uncle said something in Italian. Brando then explained, "My uncle says this was a very good place to have been sent. They cared for about 3000 patients and only 28 of them died."

"Are there any records here? Of the hospital or those who were sent to it?"

Flavio Bianchi shook his head and responded in Italian. "Unfortunately, what my uncle has told you about the hospital is all there is to learn here in Vicenza," Brando said. "The records of those who served or were treated here are part of military records—in Italy and the United States." He pointed to Beniamino's records. "This is probably everything known about your ancestor in Vicenza."

"Well, it was a long shot anyway. Thank you so much. *Grazie.* Would you let us buy the two of you lunch for your help?"

After conferring with his uncle, Brando said, "My uncle is always available for a coffee. There is a bar nearby, if you'd like."

Brea raised her eyebrows. "A bar? In the United States, a bar is a place to grab a beer or a drink after work."

Brando chuckled. "In Italy a bar is more like a café. It is popular for coffee, a brioche, even lunch, if you prefer."

As they made their way to the bar, Brando said, "Is there anything else you would like to ask? My uncle knows all about the history of this place."

"Sure," said Noah. "What makes this place special? Wait a sec. That didn't come out right."

"What are the highlights of Vicenza?" Brea said

"Yeah, what she said," added Noah.

"I will ask my uncle, if you wish, but I know his answer. And I warn you, you will be unleashing the kraken with that question. Vicenza is world famous for Andrea Palladio, the architect from the sixteenth century that gave his name to Palladian Architecture. It is classical and symmetrical, and quite beautiful. Vicenza has nearly two dozen buildings designed by Palladio. If I ask my uncle then after lunch he will want to show you those buildings and tell you about them in great detail. My Uncle Flavio … well, he can tell you more than you ever wanted to know about it. You cannot be a historian of Vicenza and not be an expert on Palladio."

"We'll take the risk. That sounds fascinating," Brea said, but turned to Noah for confirmation.

"Sure, go ahead and ask him."

. . .

On the train back to Venice, Noah said, "I'd heard of Palladian architecture, but I didn't know it was named after somebody or how to describe it."

"I didn't either. It was interesting. But Brando was right, I probably now know more about it than I ever knew there was to know, if you know what I mean."

Noah laughed. "Mom, I'm rubbing off on you. That shouldn't have made sense, but I understood every word."

"I don't think that was a compliment."

"Not really."

Brea's phone buzzed. "I've got a text from your grandpa. Hey, Noah, he found a picture of Beniamino. Take a look."

It was a black and white photo with a torn corner and a crease across Beniamino's chest. But the face was clear. "Noah, he looks like a younger version of your great-grandpa, Walter Roberts. Beniamino was Walter's dad, so it makes sense, but still."

"He looks a lot like Grandpa too—his nose and the shape of his face."

"Yeah. They all have thin lips too."

Brea sat in silence for some time, cradling her phone and the image of her ancestor—Beniamino Robustelli, a name that was becoming more and more a real person to her.

ENVELOPE #3

Traveling from Venice into Germany wasn't the hop, skip, and a jump they'd been used to. Instead of a two-hour train ride, it was an all-day affair involving layovers and multiple train transfers.

They filled the time napping, playing card games, surfing the internet on their phones, reading books, and, for Noah, writing in his notebook. He didn't offer to share anything he'd written, but Brea tried to brush it off. There was a delicate balance between privacy and hiding things, and she still didn't know where the line was. With time, she was hoping she wouldn't have to be concerned about that line.

They arrived in Fussen, Germany, tired and hungry. "I can't believe how tiring sitting all day is," Noah said. He was eating the last of the snacks they'd picked up during their layover in Munich.

Brea simply nodded, too worn out to comment. They grabbed a taxi to their hotel. Having been used to hearing Italian, and even picking up a few words, the German the driver used was jarring. When he saw their confused expressions, he switched to English.

"Where do you stay?"

Brea gave him a paper with the hotel's name and address written on it. The driver nodded and soon delivered them and their luggage to the front desk.

Hearing more German being spoken around her, Brea began to get used to the sound of it, even liking its cadence. But thankfully, the front desk clerk also spoke English. Once she checked them in, Brea said, "*Grazie*," then corrected herself by adding, "*Danke*."

Noah was busy admiring the ornate lobby and furnishings, but quickly hoisted their bags when his mom called. "Can I take the stairs?" His eyes had lit up at the sight of the sweeping, curved staircase.

"Sure. If you don't mind if I take the elevator."

"Nope. See you in a minute." He took off with an energy he'd denied having only moments before. He was standing outside the elevator doors two floors up by the time Brea arrived.

They'd opted for a traditional hotel instead of a vacation rental. It had been the easiest to arrange from Florence. The difference was they each had their own bed but not their own bedroom, and they didn't have a kitchen, rather a small mini-fridge. However, with a restaurant in the hotel, that wouldn't present a problem.

"Let's go eat," suggested Noah once they'd dumped their bags on the beds.

"Should we try the restaurant downstairs?"

"Yes, it smelled amazing."

. . .

Neuschwanstein Castle was built by "Mad" King Ludwig and was quite the sight to behold. Even though it was more Brea's thing than Noah's, they both found plenty to be fascinated with when they toured it the next day. They compared their favorite parts as they walked to the nearby luge run.

"It was so fancy. I liked exploring it, but I'd hate living in something like that," Noah said.

"I don't think you have to worry about that happening. It was very ornate, but I'm guessing any castle would probably make you feel the same way."

"Probably. But the grotto room? That was cool and weird, at the same time."

"Yeah. I liked it, but it surprised me. Who would have thought to create their own personal grotto inside a castle?"

Brea stopped short. The luge run was right in front of them, and she wasn't prepared. Their conversation had kept her mind off what they were about to do. She was a roller coaster kind of girl only in the sense that she could enjoy it knowing the tracks were tested often and were very safe. A toboggan hurtling down a hill on a shiny luge track with her in control of the only brake was another thing altogether.

For a moment, she took heart. A sign informed them the luge would not run in rainy weather. Brea glanced up at a cloudy sky then looked back at the luge operator with wide, questioning eyes.

He said, "*Was ist los?*"

Brea pointed to the sky with a shrug and hands upraised.

In response, he patted her arm reassuringly. "*Kein regen.* No rain. *Alles ist gut,*" as if that's what she wanted to hear.

"Don't worry, Mom. You're going to love it."

"Yeah, right. I think I'll love when it's over," she grumbled.

Noah laughed. "And I thought you were willing to do things I want to do that you don't." He climbed into his toboggan before Brea had a chance to respond.

She could chicken out and just let Noah take the luge run. She didn't have to do it with him. But invoking Martha's words told her that wasn't the best option. Stepping up to the luge, she was grateful to hear instructions in clear English. She gave herself an internal pep talk. "You can do this—for Noah, you can do this and follow Martha's advice one more time." She took a deep breath and then signaled for the operator to get her started. She could see the disappearing figure of Noah up ahead.

Noah's squeals of delight reached her ears as she tentatively made her way down the track. At first, she relied heavily on the hand brake. But when she realized she was slowing down the toboggans behind her, Brea made a conscious effort to relax her hand and not yank on the brake nearly as often. Before she knew it, the squeals of delight she heard were her own.

Adrenaline pumping through her, she leaped out of her sled to greet Noah at the bottom. His face broke out in a huge grin. "You liked it! You can't deny it, you liked it!"

Brea tried to suppress a smile. "I'm not sure whether to thank you or curse you. That was scary, but it was also a blast!" She bent over, trying to catch her breath. She raised a finger. "But if you think you can get me to do it again, you're seriously mistaken."

Noah chuckled. "All right."

"However, if you want to have another go, I'm content to sit here and wait for you."

As she waited for Noah to reappear down the luge run, Brea made a determination. It was time to open the third envelope. She'd had enough of doing things she didn't want to do. She was ready to follow new instructions. Surely that wouldn't be any more challenging.

. . .

Brea spotted Martha's box in her luggage as soon as they returned to their hotel. When Noah ducked into the bathroom, she had the privacy she desired to pull out the third envelope. She hesitated only briefly before carefully opening it to see what was next.

Surprisingly, Martha's directions for her appeared easy to follow. The note bore the simple instruction: *Watch Noah's face*. It did have an added note that she was to tell Noah about the contents of this envelope *after* she had done it.

But what was she watching for? And if she didn't know what she was watching for, how would she know when she had accomplished it? Maybe this instruction wasn't as easy as it first seemed.

Brea was still lost in thought when Noah emerged and caught her off guard. "What's up, Mom?"

"Umm …" She studied the paper in her hand and the open envelope in her lap.

Noah followed her gaze. "I see. Finally opened it, huh?" He had an amused note to his voice. He opened his mouth to say more then shut it instead. "I'm starving. Let's go eat."

Over dinner at a nearby restaurant, Brea kept thinking about watching Noah's face. She found herself staring at him, but whenever he caught her, she averted her gaze.

Noah's was the most familiar face she knew. She'd seen it every day since the day he was born except for the few days he was away at summer camp. Unlike her own face, she didn't have to gaze in a mirror to see it, she just needed to look in front of her. And when he wasn't in front of her, he was in the forefront of her mind. What could she be watching for that she didn't already see and hadn't been seeing for years?

Watch Noah's face? And wasn't that what she'd been doing on this trip? Noah had finally loosened up enough to let his guard down, and she'd been able to read him like she used to. Martha must have known how Noah had been hiding things from her, hiding himself from her. But she couldn't have known that her earlier instructions would have already produced these results. Maybe this bit of instruction was already finished.

"So, what are we doing tomorrow?"

His question shook her out of her reverie. "What?"

"Tomorrow? Where are we headed tomorrow?" They'd all but ditched their preplanned itinerary.

"Oh, yeah. Well, since we're here in Germany, I was investigating what we could do. We could go to Munich. They have a ton of museums, an aquarium, … Here, I bookmarked them on my phone." She scrolled through the options with him. "Or we could rent a car and drive up the Romantic Road. It wends its way through picturesque towns and past a number of castles. We could stop in Rothenberg. It's supposed to be the quintessential medieval Bavarian town."

"Sure. Either of those sounds fine."

Brea was about to pin him down to which he would prefer when she stopped listening to his words and paid attention to his face instead. The excitement she'd seen earlier in the day was gone. His face was now a blank slate, a perfect picture of indifference.

"Noah, how about we just head to France, to Viborgne?" Without staring too obviously, she watched his face. The light came back into his eyes.

Outwardly, he tried to act nonchalant. He casually shrugged. "That would work too. Whatever you'd like." But Brea saw the change that came over him, however briefly. He had visibly perked up—his head held straighter, his mouth involuntarily smiling, the light from his eyes spreading across his entire face. It was there and then gone behind a mask he pulled down over it as he dropped his gaze. She had been watching his face lately to gauge how much he was enjoying their sightseeing, but she hadn't really compared his words to his face to see if they matched up. It's not like she was detecting lies, rather getting to the bottom of emotions he wasn't willing to admit to.

"Noah, look at me a minute, will you?"

He lifted his head. "What?"

"Are you ready? Do you know what you want to do in Viborgne? Have you done enough research?"

He stared at her, struggling to hide his emotions. Finally, he subtly nodded. "I'm ready," he said quietly.

"Okay, then. We better get back so I can book train tickets to France for tomorrow."

Noah had a hard time hiding his excitement. "Okay. Let's do it."

. . .

With the prospect of another all-day train trip in front of them, Brea and Noah spent the rest of their evening preparing. By the time they embarked on the first leg of their journey the next morning, they had charged-up computers and phones and had plenty of supplies. The staff at the hotel had been very helpful. For a reasonable price, they'd found a disposable cooler for Brea and Noah and filled it with ice packs and enough food to last them two days. Brea and Noah used their limited German vocabulary, mostly *bitte* and *danke*, again and again in the process.

Taking advantage of the train's Wi-Fi, Brea spent the morning catching up on work emails she'd been neglecting since the beginning of their trip. Noah was working silently beside her on his laptop.

As she finished the last of her emails, she glanced at her growing child beside her. He was intently staring at his screen, his brow knit in deep concentration. Other than last night when asking about plans, when was the last time she'd really looked at him, watched his face, discerned the subtle changes in his mood? Sure, she'd noticed him more on this trip than she had in a long time, but she'd attributed that to him dropping his guard and relaxing more. But even last night he'd tried to hide his true feelings. If she hadn't been watching, carefully watching, she wouldn't have caught it.

Despite him being a teenager, it was easy to assume she already knew him, that he was an open book to her, that somehow regardless of how closed he appeared, she could still see through all that. But clearly, that wasn't the case. She hadn't any clue that he'd lost his friends. She didn't know he'd started writing. What else didn't she know? What could she learn if she took the time to watch and listen?

Noah abruptly lifted his head from his screen, startling Brea. "Mom?" He gave her a sideways glance. "What's up? Why are you staring at me?"

"I'm sorry. I was watching your face."

"What?"

"The third envelope—it said: *Watch Noah's face.*"

Noah immediately wiped his face of emotion, wary.

"Don't do that. Martha gave me that advice, but she told me not to tell you until after I'd done it. I guess I figured over time I knew you inside and out, that I didn't need to keep learning who you are. But Martha, even from beyond the grave, pointed out my error."

"So … is that a good thing?"

"Of course it is. You're still a work in progress."

"I guess I can live with that. But I thought you weren't supposed to tell me until after you'd done it. Watching me on the train for five minutes was it?"

"No. Watching your face is why we're here on this train heading to Paris and onto Château-Thierry, where we'll be staying." Noah looked puzzled. "When I suggested we check out other places in Germany, your face fell. It didn't match your words. It really is okay to tell me what you think, Noah. I may not always agree with you, and the decision may not always go your way. But if you tell me your thoughts then I can take them into account."

He regarded her a moment. "Okay, I'll try, but you know it's not that easy, right?"

"Yeah, I do. But I'll take your, 'I'll try.'"

"All right. Actually, I do want to tell you something."

Brea stiffened, not knowing what he meant by that. "What?"

Noah chuckled. "Talk about watching *my* face. You should see *yours*." He laughed some more. "Don't worry. It's not that kind of thing. I wanted to tell you what I figured out."

"Oh," Brea said with a sigh of relief. "Sorry about that. I guess you've been looking up Viborgne. Did you learn something?"

"No. Quite honestly, I know almost nothing more about Viborgne. Regardless of how much I research, I don't learn anything new. But I'm ready to go there because I think the only place to learn about Viborgne is Viborgne." He shrugged. "I was actually googling something else and emailing Matteo and Carlo."

"Oh? How are they?"

"They're great." With a side eye, he added, "They enjoyed hearing how much you loved the luge run."

"You didn't!"

"Maybe I did, and maybe I didn't. But they thought you were both brave and hilarious."

Brea pretended to be angry but her face kept undoing her efforts. She finally gave up. "So, you had to make a point to tell me that?"

"No, not really—just a bonus." He grinned. "What I was googling was the hospital in Vicenza."

"Really?"

"Yeah. Great-Great-Grandpa Robustelli was discharged in November 1918, right? And that's when the hospital started shutting down because the war ended. It took them a few months to have it completely closed, but that freed up most of the staff. I read that some of the nurses traveled around Europe a bit before heading back to the United States in the spring of 1919. That got me thinking. Beniamino's Ellis Island record said he showed up in 1919, wasn't it May of 1919?"

"Yeah, I think so."

"What did he do between November 1918 and when he got on the ship to America? The nurses went and played tourist. Why didn't he go home to Orvieto?"

"Maybe he did."

"I don't think so, other than maybe a quick visit goodbye. Remember his Ellis Island record says his last permanent residence was Vicenza. Being in a hospital for a few months doesn't seem like a permanent residence. Why didn't he put down his hometown, Orvieto? Why didn't he return to Orvieto?"

"Those are great questions."

"And why was he in Vicenza in the first place? The hospital served Americans and Italians that came from the nearby Italian front. But Great-Great-Grandpa was in France, wasn't he?"

"You're right. That's what his service record said. But we don't know what errand he was on or why he was there."

"Exactly." He gave her a sly grin. "It looks like you've got a mystery on your hands just like I do."

Brea nodded. "So, I do. Thanks for your help. Maybe if you keep helping me and I help you, we can solve at least one of them. Deal?"

"Deal. But I think you should choose the 'phone-a-friend' option. Maybe Grandpa can search for records in the United States and see if there's more information."

"That's a great idea. I will."

. . .

They were worn out by the time they'd made all their train transfers, arrived in Château-Thierry, taken a cab to their hotel, and dumped their bags on their beds. But Brea had not forgotten Noah's suggestion. It was early afternoon back in the States when she reached her dad by phone.

"Hi, Dad."

"Hi, Brea! Are you okay?"

"Yes, of course," she said, taken aback. "Were you worried that I wasn't?"

"Not until you called. You've texted but never called before. From Europe, I mean."

"Sorry about that. We're fine. Thanks for the picture of my great-grandfather. I'm trying to track down more information about him. He was in the U.S. Army Base Hospital 102 in Vicenza, Italy, at the end of the war when he was discharged. That was in November 1918. It seems he left from Vicenza to go to the United States, arriving at Ellis Island in May 1919. We don't know what happened to him between November and May. And we don't know the nature of his stay in the hospital. We've checked things out from this end without learning much. Can you see what you can find there? From U.S. Army records or maybe in his personal papers?"

"Sure. I found that photo, didn't I? I'll see what I can dig up."

They chatted for a few more minutes before Noah's rumbling stomach reminded Brea she had other things to take care of. "Thanks, Dad. Love you."

"Love you too."

ENVELOPE #4

Château-Thierry was home to significant World War I activity. Hopefully by starting there, Brea and Noah could learn more about the involvement of nearby Viborgne. Brea rented a car first thing in the morning to allow them flexibility in coming and going.

On a hill two miles west of town was the Château-Thierry American Monument. Despite waning interest in World War I, a large visitor's center had been constructed 100 years after the main events had taken place there. At the base of the nearby Belleau Wood was a large cemetery with a sweeping circle of white crosses marking the graves of over 2000 war dead.

Brea and Noah strolled among these somber settings, learning more of the Battle of Château-Thierry. The newly arrived American Expeditionary Forces under General "Black Jack" Pershing engaged in battle against the Germans on the 31st of May, 1918. A few days later, the U.S. Army and Marine Corps joined forces with their French allies, forcing the Germans back across the Marne River. The ensuing bloody skirmishes in Belleau Wood went on into July. It was a significant opportunity for the American forces to prove their worth, later being recognized as a turning point in the war.

The two of them sat on the steps of the monument quietly discussing what they'd learned. It had been a humbling and sobering day. "I can't help thinking about all those mothers who would never see their sons again or those wives whose husbands would never return."

"Or sons who would grow up without fathers," Noah added.

Brea turned at his words. "I forget how real that is for you sometimes. Is it hard for you to be here?"

Noah shrugged. "Not because of Dad. War is just sad."

"Noah, you forget I'm watching your face. Let me suggest you never play poker. You don't have the face for it."

He threw up his arms. "If Mimi were here, I'd have a few choice words for her. She figured out that my whole face is my tell. And if she hadn't told you ..." He sounded angry, but his gentle smile revealed the truth.

Brea laid her hand on top of Noah's and turned to gaze out over the valley below them. "I would have two words for her—thank you."

Noah leaned his head on his mother's shoulder. "Yeah, I guess, me too."

The drive back to their hotel was a quiet one with much to contemplate. But by the time they returned, Brea had one thought that had overtaken all others—nothing they had seen or read mentioned Viborgne.

. . .

"Noah, do you want to drive out to Viborgne while there's still daylight? We may not be able to do much, but it would be a start." A fierce determination to help Noah find answers about Viborgne was building inside her.

"No, that's okay. Tomorrow will be soon enough." His voice didn't carry the enthusiasm Brea expected.

"Are you sure? Is everything okay?"

"Yeah, I'm fine."

Brea stared at his face. It was blank. She was kicking herself for revealing she was watching his face because now he was being cautious with his expressions. Apparently, the whole mothering thing was a work in progress, like Noah himself was. She sighed. "Well, in that case, I think I'll take a nap."

"Okay. There's a patio off the lobby downstairs. Is it okay if I hang out there while you're sleeping?"

"Sure."

When Brea woke up, the sun was sliding down the sky. She stretched before noticing Noah had not returned to the room. She found him a few minutes later on the patio he had mentioned. His blue notebook was open on the table in front of him.

"Hi, Mom. How was your nap?"

"Helpful. I didn't realize how much everything was catching up with me. Have you been here this whole time?"

"Yep." He glanced at his notebook but made no effort to shut it like he often did. "I've been thinking and writing."

"Good pastimes. Were they productive?" It was a leading question. She hoped he'd open up more but was still trying to let it be his choice.

He didn't answer her question, instead having one of his own. "Mom, why are we here?"

"In Château-Thierry? In France?"

"Yeah, why?"

"Because you wanted to find George Harrison." The answer seemed way too obvious. "Am I missing something?"

"Maybe. Maybe you're missing a whole lot of things. We could still be in Germany. So, why are we here in France?" His voice was rising in agitation.

"Because you wanted to come here. You said you were ready." She reached to put a hand on his arm, but he brushed it aside. "What are you getting at, Noah? What's wrong?"

"Do you always do what *I* want?"

"No, but I'm trying to do things that you want that I don't want to do, remember? I thought that was a good thing."

He huffed and folded his arms. "If it weren't for Mimi's envelope, would you have done it anyway?"

Brea thought back over her decisions of late. Would she have still brought Noah to Europe like he wanted? Probably. She thought about opening up to Noah and answering his questions, about climbing the Leaning Tower of Pisa and riding the luge in Germany. "To be honest, Noah, I don't know if I would have talked to you about my dating or the lack thereof, but I'm pretty sure I would have brought you to Europe. I would have even climbed that tower and ridden that sled." She pulled up a chair next to him. "Are you worried that I spoil you? Is that it? Is that why you were googling Vicenza and your great-great-grandpa? For me, out of guilt?"

"No, not really to any of that. Or maybe. I don't know. I'm getting interested in Beniamino's story too, but I can't say that guilt wasn't part of what prompted me to look him up. And I don't think you spoil me, or at least I won't admit to it if you do. You set plenty of limits as a mom." He paused and frowned. "But if something is important to me, you find a way to make it happen, even if you have to sacrifice to do it." He didn't mean it as a compliment.

"So … I'm supposed to feel bad that I'm doing things for you? That doesn't make any sense, Noah. Besides, I've been enjoying this trip too. And we spent all that time researching Benjamin Roberts—before you cared about him."

Noah didn't appear convinced. He raised an eyebrow and made no attempt to conceal his skepticism.

"Maybe I do put your needs before my own. I'm a mom, Noah. That's what we do."

"I know, but …"

"But, what?"

"Here, maybe I can explain it differently. I opened the fourth envelope." He handed a slip of paper to her.

Brea read silently: *Share a poem you've written (or write a new one) and tell your mom what it means.*

"A poem? Noah, you write poetry too?"

He shrugged. "Yeah, I do. I'd planned to keep that to myself, but I guess once you tell Mimi, you tell the world."

Brea nodded her head. "She's kind of a bossy old broad from the other side, isn't she?"

Noah laughed. "I can't believe you called her that."

"Yeah. Don't tell her, okay? 'Cause I happen to love and miss that old broad."

"Yeah. Me too."

"So, the poem …"

"Okay. It's a new one. I've written others, but I came down here to the patio to see if I could put together a new one. Here goes."

Shadows
A ghost walks among us
Unseen yet casting shadows upon our lives
Ghoul or guardian, it's hard to tell
At once one, then soon another
> *She does double duty so you do not miss him*
> *But how can you miss what you do not know?*

A stranger walks among us
Hero, larger than life, yet vastly human too
Stories told at grandma's knee
Or once, but now no longer
> *She has tried so hard to make him known*
> *But how can you know what you cannot see?*

A woman walks among us
Filling holes, being both, though only one
Eclipsed by shadows allowed to hang
Not once, but over and again
He yearns for her to shine, to know she is enough
But how can she see that she has yet to be?

They sat quietly after Noah finished reading. Brea moved her chair closer and put her arm around her son. "That was beautiful. I don't think you need to tell me what it means. I understand."

He turned to scrutinize her. "I'm not sure you do. Mom, I know it's been hard to be a single mom, but that's just half of it. It's like you're always in Dad's shadow because of the circumstances of his death, or his life, for that matter. And you're busy playing a role for someone else. You're the wife of the hero *and* the villain. You're both Mom and Dad. But I don't think you're ever *you.*

"I want to know my dad, but there's only so much I *can* know. I'll never know what it's like to go out in the backyard and play football with him. I'll never see him beam proudly when I graduate from college." He shook his head to clear his thoughts. "Grandma used to tell me stories about him, but she doesn't do that much anymore. I think partly it's because I'm too old to snuggle on her lap, but I think it's more because only a set number of stories to tell existed in the first place. He's not alive to add new material. But maybe what I know is enough or should be. I need to accept that, and, I think, so do you."

He sighed and looked directly at his mom. "I think Dad's shadow is unfinished business for both of us. I've learned to be more proud than ashamed of Dad because of Mimi. I don't want to always be chasing a shadow that can't be captured or held or felt. But what I want more than that is for you to be free. You can have a life. Do you realize that?"

Brea nodded in agreement, but she said nothing. Her only thought was, *Yes, but can I really?*

ENVELOPE #5

The next morning, they arose early. But before they left for Viborgne, Noah had a suggestion. "Mom, when I pulled out my envelope, I saw the next one underneath it. It's addressed to both of us. I say we don't wait. Let's open it."

"Okay, why don't you grab it. You can read it to me in the car on the way to Viborgne." She wasn't sure how she might react to a letter they were both reading at the same time. Driving, with her eyes on the road, might allow her to keep her emotions in check.

"All right, Mom, should I open it?" Noah asked once they were on their way.

"Yes. I'm ready." She hoped she was.

Noah laughed before he read it out loud. "It says *Have an adventure together.* I think we've got that one down."

"Yeah. I think we're already doing that."

Suddenly, the car lurched and Brea steered it quickly to the side of the road. Climbing out, they discovered a very flat, right, rear tire. "I guess I spoke too soon. Let's see what we can do about this."

With only a little bit of effort they located the spare, but it was a compact spare which didn't instill a great deal of confidence in Brea. "Noah, before we change this, let me call the rental company. Maybe they have a better option."

Maybe they had a better option, and maybe they didn't. Although Brea and Noah had taken the time to pick up a few French words such as *merci* and *s'il vous plait*, they hadn't thought to look up the French words for flat tire.

While Brea tried to convey their need to the operator, Noah pulled out his phone and began translating words for his mother. She didn't know how to pronounce what appeared on the screen, but she tried her best. Soon Noah simply opted for the voice translations which they held up to Brea's phone.

Finally, an exclamation of, "*Oui, oui,*" came through Brea's phone. But how could they convey their location? Noah and Brea glanced around for any road signs or landmarks, to no avail.

A Frenchman drove by, slowing down to stare at them. Brea made eye contact with him and silently pleaded for help. He drove past much to her dismay, but a short distance ahead, he pulled off to the side of the road. Slowly, he got out of his truck and made his way back to the pair.

Brea pointed to the flat tire, showed him the rental car contract, then handed the phone to him. He peered at it suspiciously, but took it and put it to his ear. A grin spread across his face, and he started conversing rapidly in French.

As he talked, Brea and Noah leaned against the rental car. "Thank goodness he came along."

"No kidding," Noah said, but he was smiling.

"Why are you happy?"

"Well, you have to admit this is quite the adventure we're having. At least we're not dealing with this alone. I don't mind so much when we're sharing the experience."

"Martha did say we should have the adventure together. You know, the whole misery loves company."

"Oh, so we can both be miserable together and complain together."

Brea laughed. "It does come across like that, doesn't it?"

"I think the saying should be: *Misery with company isn't as miserable.*"

"I like that."

Noah reached into the back seat of the car and retrieved his notebook from his backpack. "I've got to write that one down before I forget it."

While Noah wrote, the Frenchman returned and handed Brea's phone back. Brea wasn't sure what all his gestures meant, but she got the idea that they should stay put.

"So, what did he say, Mom?"

"I'm not sure, but he pointed to his watch. I think he was showing me half an hour, but …" She shrugged. "Are you up for hanging out here for thirty minutes or so? Or we could put on the spare and limp on our way."

"If someone's coming, I don't want to leave."

"I had the same thought. I didn't want to ditch someone who might come all the way out here."

They passed the time pointing out the beauties of the French countryside around them, telling jokes, and recounting their new favorite foods they would miss once they returned home. When a tow truck pulled up actually about a half hour later, Brea realized how easy it had been to talk with Noah. They hadn't talked about any substantive issues like she'd hoped for lately, but before this trip began, she'd just hoped he would talk to her again—about anything, big or small, it didn't matter. And that's exactly what they were doing.

Lost in these thoughts, she hadn't noticed Noah and the tow truck driver talking while examining the tire. After a moment, the driver returned to his truck and Noah came over to her.

"What did he say?"

"I have no idea."

"What? I thought you two were lost in conversation."

"Oh no, not at all. He pulled me over and started talking to me. I just nodded every once in a while. But I have no idea what he said."

They waited ten minutes, fifteen minutes, but the driver stayed in his truck the whole time. "Do you think he's waiting for us to do something, offer him money or something?"

Noah shrugged. "He didn't put his hand out, but …"

Brea finally determined to attempt a conversation with the driver. Walking toward his truck, she heard Noah call her. "Mom! Come back."

She turned around. A car similar to their rental car was pulling up behind theirs. A woman in the uniform of the rental company got out.

"I am sorry for your trouble. We brought you a new car."

"Thank you, but the man …" Brea pointed in the other direction at the tow truck.

The woman blushed. "Yes. That is my husband. He will put on the spare after you leave, and then he will follow me as I drive the car back to the office to make sure all is safe. He didn't want to make you wait alone. He is very protective. I am sorry."

"Oh, no need to apologize. I think I understand about protective men." She winked at Noah.

They moved their belongings to the new rental and were on their way in no time. Since they had started early, the delay merely wasted some time but did not cost them the day.

Viborgne was a small town that appeared as if nothing new had been built there since long before either world war, although surely that was not the case. As Brea navigated the narrow streets, Noah swiveled all around, taking in as much as possible.

"I saw a few pictures online of what the town looked like, but it's so much better in person. Did you see those colorful shutters and the arched doorways?"

They both marveled at the charming city that time seemed to have forgotten. "Should we start at the church?" Brea could see its steeple peeking above the buildings and trees ahead.

"No. I thought about the church at first. But we're not looking for birth records or anything like that. We need to go through the newspaper archives. There's a town hall not far from the church. That's where I want to start."

"Okay. Tell me how to get there, and that's where we'll go."

A short time later, Brea and Noah were hunched around an old computer in a side office of the town hall. From what they gathered, the old newspapers had been partially digitized. What part was digitized and what wasn't, they had been unable to ascertain.

The elderly town clerk had been reluctant to let them use the computer by themselves, but when he saw the picture of a laptop on Brea's business card, that was enough to convince him they knew what they were doing. As he walked out leaving them alone, he let out a sigh of relief.

"I think that guy doesn't know much about computers. I'm pretty sure he's assuming you know more than he does."

"Yeah, well, he's probably not wrong." Brea grimaced. "The problem is I think I know a lot more than whoever set up this database. The search function alone is terrible. I can put in a date or a topic, but I can't put in both together. And then, you have to click through five or six screens before you even learn if what you're looking for is online or on microfiche. And if it's on microfiche, you have to exit out of this and go to a different registry altogether to find where it is."

Noah plopped down beside her, deflated. "Is it even worth trying?"

"It's difficult but not hopeless. I'm not giving up yet. Just keep your phone handy for translating. Having it all in French does not help the situation."

Two hours later, hot, sweaty, and discouraged, Brea pushed back from the computer. "Okay, looking for George Harrison just brings up information about the Beatles. Since I can't add the date to the search, that got us nowhere."

"Yeah, and searching for Hero of Viborgne was a joke. I hadn't thought about everything being about Viborgne, and apparently, they have a lot of heroes here. They're mostly local boys though."

"I'm guessing our best bet is picking meticulously through everything in 1918. Since the Americans showed up around May, according to what we learned at Château-Thierry, that would narrow things down. Do you want to try that?"

He didn't answer, but the plaintive look on his face was enough. They couldn't have come all this way not to find answers.

"Well, it's way past lunchtime. Would you mind venturing out on your own to grab us something to eat? I noticed a small market a few doors down. Maybe bread and cheese? I can start working through the records while you're gone."

"Sure."

By the time Noah returned, Brea was completely discouraged. The majority of the records back that far were still on microfiche, and most entries in the database were for entire daily editions of the paper instead of listings of the individual stories. They would need to hire a native French speaker to read through entire editions of the newspapers to find anything.

"I'm not sure what to tell you, Noah," she said after explaining the problem.

"Maybe we can ask the clerk if there are other options?"

"It certainly won't hurt. But let's eat first. I'm starving."

They didn't know if eating in the computer room was permitted, but no one had told them not to, so they hungrily devoured the bread, cheese, and fruit Noah bought. "I'm going to let you do the shopping more often. That was delicious."

"Thanks, but I think anything would have tasted good at this point."

"True," Brea agreed. "Let's clean up and go talk to the clerk."

The old clerk who had helped them when they first arrived in the late morning spoke a little bit of English. The afternoon clerk appeared to be even more ancient, if that was possible, and didn't speak a word of English.

"I didn't know we'd gotten so lucky this morning," Noah whispered to his mom.

Brea didn't respond. She was too busy googling French phrases, showing them to the clerk, and hoping he would find a way to respond. It was not going well.

"Mom, remember the guy's nephew in Vicenza? Maybe we can find someone like that who speaks English. We definitely need help."

"That's a great idea, but how do we find someone? Just go out on the street and start asking random strangers?"

"No." Then Noah's face lit up. "I'll be right back."

Brea and the clerk glanced at each other, perplexed, as Noah tore out the door. Brea shrugged in response to the clerk's raised eyebrows, then they waited in silence until Noah returned a short time later.

"Mom, this is the guy from the market who helped me pick out the bread and cheese. His English is pretty good." Standing beside Noah was a young man, tall and slim. He had a crop of dark hair on his head and a thin mustache on his upper lip. He was wearing a t-shirt with the name Le Marché de la Ville emblazoned on the front. Even though he was smiling, he seemed bewildered.

Brea sighed in relief, but they all turned at the even bigger sigh from the town clerk. Brea tried to stifle a laugh when the clerk burst out laughing himself.

"Well," Brea said to the newcomer, "I'm glad you're here. We should have learned more French before we came. That's on us. But we're here now. I'm Brea. This is Noah. Thank you so much for coming."

"Hello. My name is Hugo."

"Nice to meet you, Hugo. Can you help us with some French? This clerk seems nice, but he doesn't speak English, and we don't speak French."

"Yes, of course. What do you need?"

Noah jumped in with, "We're looking through old records back around World War I, but we're not making much progress with the computer database. We were wondering if there are other options."

Hugo nodded. He and the clerk, whose name they learned was Henri, carried on a conversation for several minutes. Near the end of it, Henri grew animated and grinned broadly.

"What did he say?" Noah said, hopeful and eager.

"He says you should speak to Monsieur Etienne. He will remember."

Noah was excited, but Brea wasn't. "I appreciate that, but we're not talking about World War II. We're looking for information from 1918, around the time of World War I. He wouldn't have been alive to remember back that far."

Hugo knit his brow and again spoke to Henri. Turning back to the Americans, he said, "He insists. Henri said, 'No, no, he is … *excentrique*.' Do you understand this word?"

"Eccentric?"

"Yes, that's it. Henri told me, 'He will remember.' I don't know what that means, but that's what he said."

"Okay," Brea said with a great deal of skepticism. "I have no clue how being eccentric is going to help us, but I don't think we have a better option. How can we speak with Mister, or I should say Monsieur, Etienne? And do we need to hire an interpreter?"

With the help of Hugo and Henri, and after a short phone call, a meeting had been set up for the next day with Alexandre Etienne. And although Brea was doubtful, Henri, by way of Hugo, assured her Monsieur Etienne spoke English.

"Well, that turned out differently than I expected," Brea said as they emerged from the town hall.

"Yeah. At least we haven't hit a dead end yet. I'm happy about that."

"Me too. Do you want to walk around the town a bit? It's getting close to dinner time, but we did just eat a late lunch. We could grab dinner here or back in Château-Thierry. What would you like?"

Noah looked a little sheepish. "I'm still hungry, but I could wait a little while for you to be ready for dinner. I suppose we could walk around town in the meantime."

Brea grinned. "Why don't we go back to the market. Maybe Hugo could help you find something to tide you over."

Hugo, once again, helped them more than they could have expected. He loaded them up with bread and pastries made fresh for the market by a local bakery. Then he directed them to a nearby restaurant, even writing down the French names of dishes they might enjoy. He described the dishes with such rapture on his face that Brea decided she was hungry after all.

After thanking Hugo profusely, and even taking a selfie with him, they returned to their car to drop off their purchases. They gradually strolled to the restaurant, enjoying the feel of the town and the sound of the French being spoken around them.

. . .

It was a relief to arrive safely back at their hotel that night. Driving back, they both turned their heads to stare at the side of the road where they'd been waylaid that morning, although neither said anything.

Dropping onto his bed, Noah said, "Do you think that was enough of an adventure?"

"I sure hope so. But you were right, it wasn't so bad doing it together."

Noah smiled. "I guess maybe we can manage this life thing, right? Doing it together?"

"I like the sound of that."

"So, do you know where this guy lives that we're going to meet tomorrow?"

"Not yet." Brea pulled out her laptop to look up his address. "From what Hugo was saying, it sounds like he lives on the outskirts of town. I think we should print out directions in case there's no cell coverage. And despite the assurance that Monsieur Etienne speaks English, I think we should find a French-English dictionary. Again, I'm not sure our phones will have reliable service where we're headed. It's also clear the few French phrases and words we've picked up are totally useless."

The directions seemed easy enough. After printing them using the hotel's printer, Brea checked her email. The only one of interest was from her dad.

"Hey, Noah. Your grandpa found more out about Beniamino." She was skimming the email. "He says, 'Yes, he was at the hospital in Vicenza.' But we already knew that. Let me read you the rest. It says, 'I didn't get anywhere with the United States records about the base hospital. There's got to be a way to get to those, but I have no idea what it is. What I did find was my grandfather's journal.'"

"Oh, that's cool. I didn't know he wrote a journal," said Noah.

"Apparently, none of us did. But let me read you the rest. 'He was horrible about writing in it, and his handwriting is hard to decipher. On top of that, it's written in a mixture of Italian and French. Later he switched to English. It's sketchy, but he did say he was shot in France in July of 1918. He was treated there but wasn't healing very fast. So, when the United States opened a base hospital in Vicenza, much closer to home, he was transferred there. The next entry after that was when he was on the boat heading to America in May. He wrote in English and was really excited. But he didn't say anything about what he was busy doing between his discharge and then.'"

"That explains how he ended up in Vicenza, but other than that, it didn't tell us a whole lot we didn't already know," Noah said.

"I know. I'd like to see the whole journal when we get back home."

"Yeah, me too."

"Really?"

"Yeah. I told you I want to know about George Harrison, but my own ancestor's story is pretty interesting too."

"It is, isn't it?"

AN AMERICAN MARINE

When Brea woke up the next morning, a text was waiting from her dad. "Found my grandmother's journal—Hazel, who was Benjamin's wife. It's the same handwriting from the Bible. Her journal is more detailed and with better handwriting than his. I haven't read much yet. I'll let you know if she writes anything about her husband and his history in Italy."

Brea didn't realize she'd audibly cheered until Noah sat up in bed. "What's up, Mom?"

"Sorry. I didn't mean to wake you."

"That's okay, but what happened?"

"I got a text from your grandpa. Beniamino's wife was Hazel. He found her journal. He doesn't know if it will tell us anything about Italy yet, but he'll read it and keep us posted."

"That's great." Noah was fully awake now. "So, what should we do this morning?"

"Our appointment with M. Etienne isn't until 1:00. So, let's have a nice breakfast and pick up a French-English dictionary. Then we could head out to Viborgne on the early side. You know, just in case …"

"Right. In case we have another adventure. I also downloaded an app on my phone last night specifically for translating between French and English. But like you said, we may not have cell service."

"Good thinking."

. . .

It turns out they were better prepared than they needed to be. To start with, they arrived an hour early. So, after locating Monsieur Etienne's residence, they retreated to the main part of town to grab lunch. They thought of returning to the restaurant from the previous evening, but there was no guarantee their lunch would arrive quickly enough to allow them to return on time. So, instead, they visited their favorite market, Le Marché de la Ville.

They heard, "Hello, Noah. Hello, Brea," as soon as they entered.

"Hi, Hugo. It's good to see you again. Are you always working?" Brea said.

Hugo grinned. "My parents don't think I work enough. This is their market."

"Oh, that makes sense."

"Do you like working here?" Noah asked.

"Yes, I do. As long as I don't have to work too hard." Hugo winked.

They again bought fruit and bread. Hugo also convinced them to try some cheeses with names they'd never heard before. Then he pointed out nearby benches in the town square where they could sit and enjoy their lunch.

Noah took a big bite of a veined bleu cheese and immediately spit it out. "Yuck! What was Hugo thinking?"

Brea burst out laughing. Noah narrowed his eyes at her. "You think that's funny? Then you try it."

"Okay, okay," Brea said as she wiped her eyes. "Just let me stop laughing." She took the cheese Noah offered and attempted to take a small nibble.

"Nope, a real bite."

"Hey, it's not my fault you took a big bite," Brea said as she quickly took a tiny taste. "Hmm. That's not bad. It's strong, but I like it."

"You would," Noah said, trying to act disgruntled.

"Here. I'll take a big bite of one of the other cheeses. You pick which one."

The problem Noah discovered was, despite wanting to find the worst possible cheese for his mother, the others didn't even have strong smells. He finally chose the cheese with the darkest color.

Brea hesitated only slightly. "Here goes." She opened her mouth wide and closed her eyes. As the flavor hit, she opened her eyes in wonder. "Wow. That's really good."

"That is so not fair," Noah mumbled. He picked up an apple and bit into it.

"Hey, you're eating an apple. You know, you're the apple–"

"I know, I know. I'm the apple of your eye. I'm also your guinea pig, apparently."

Brea ruffled his hair. "Love you, kiddo."

"Love you too," he whispered back.

It was a little thing, but it was the biggest thing he'd said to his mom in a very long time.

. . .

After eating, they returned to M. Etienne's house to discover they were overprepared in the language department as well. The French to English app Noah downloaded was fully operational as their cell service was strong. The dictionary they'd found was easy to use. Most importantly, however, was the fact that Monsieur Etienne spoke excellent English—heavily accented but excellent all the same.

"Hello, Monsieur Etienne, my name is Brea Cass. This is my son, Noah."

"Yes, yes. I've been expecting you. I am Alexandre Etienne." He was an elderly gentleman. What hair he had left was pure white and lay in gentle wisps across his head. His skin was bronzed, not surprising given the well-tended flower garden in front of his house. He had a cane, but he didn't lean on it, rather swung it back and forth like a toy. "Welcome, welcome to my home. I am so happy to see you."

"Merci. We appreciate you taking time to talk with us."

"It is always a pleasure to see Americans, but we do not see people of your nationality much here. Our small town is not the typical tourist trap."

"You don't get people coming over from Château-Thierry?" Noah said.

"No. Viborgne took some damage in the war because we were in close proximity, but nothing significant. The battle was there not here. Why would they come out of their way to see Viborgne?"

"Yeah, I guess you're right."

"Monsieur Etienne, your English is excellent. How did you come to learn English? I'm pleased but surprised," Brea asked.

He chuckled lightly. "You mean since I am an old man living in an isolated French village?"

"I didn't mean …" Brea ended up shrugging. "I'm sorry, but I guess so."

He patted her shoulder. "It's okay. No one in town understands why I bothered to learn either. Come on into my study to sit down, and I will tell you." He swung his cane to point the way. "But first, I will get us something to drink."

When they were all settled in his cozy den, each with a cup of tea, Monsieur Etienne got a nostalgic look in his eye. "You asked why I learned English. I will tell you. My father insisted. I have been speaking English since I was a small child."

"Really? That's amazing."

"Yes. It is on account of the Hero of Viborgne."

Noah nearly spit his tea across the room. "Can you say that again?"

"The Hero of Viborgne? Is this a problem? Have I upset you?"

"No," Brea assured him, her hands nearly shaking. "You haven't upset us. What you said startled us."

"That's why we're here. We came to learn about the Hero of Viborgne. He's the father of our old neighbor." Noah was struggling to contain his excitement. "But are you talking about the same hero we are? There are a lot of heroes. We learned that trying to search through Viborgne's newspaper archives."

"Yes. I doubt we would be talking about the same person. But, for me, there is only one Hero of Viborgne. He was an American, the only person I know worthy of such a title."

"That could be him," Noah said, breathless with excitement. "Whatever our guy did happened in 1918. Is that the same person you're thinking of?"

M. Etienne grew quiet and misty eyed. "Yes. 1918." A few moments of silence passed before he could compose himself enough to continue. "My father was eight years old in 1918. There was much fighting that summer in Château-Thierry and Belleau Wood. His family could smell the smoke from the guns and lived with the constant percussion of their artillery. Some errant bombing damaged the steeple of our church, but thankfully none of our homes. My grandmother finally one afternoon in frustration packed away anything glass in straw and sawdust—pictures on the walls that were covered with glass, goblets, figurines. She said the constant shaking was certain to break them all. When I was little, she would put me on her knee and show me the wine glasses that survived. She would say, 'Sawdust may not seem like much, but for glass, it is more powerful than guns.' My father would shake his head because she said it so often. Sometimes, he would mumble, 'Don't tell someone who's in front of a firing squad such a silly thing.' But he would beam too. He was proud of his mama for being resourceful."

Alexandre walked over to a nearby shelf and took down two seemingly identical glasses. He handed one to each of them. "If you look closely, one of them has a very small crack near the stem. I spotted it as a child, but I never dared to tell my grandma."

Tipping the goblets up and comparing them, Noah finally spotted the fissure. "There it is. You must have seen it as a child because you were staring up at the glass from the underside."

Alexandre nodded and grinned. "A very clever young man. Yes, you are right." He collected the glassware and carefully replaced it on the shelf before returning to his chair and his tale.

"But you did not come to hear an old man grow nostalgic about sawdust, did you?"

"No, sir, but I liked the story. I never thought about what it would be like to live in the middle of a war."

"No, son, you should be grateful for not knowing such things. My homeland has been the scene of great conflicts. While the cause being fought for and the freedoms being preserved can be important, war is never pretty. But I will no longer delay the story you want to hear.

"When my father was eight, as I was saying, war was raging nearby. One afternoon, an American marine came to town scrounging for food."

"Was his name George Harrison?" Noah eagerly interrupted.

"I do not know his name. I imagine my father did, but that was never shared with me. He was always just The Hero. But … I do have his picture."

Brea and Noah both held their breath while Alexandre retrieved an old photograph stashed near the World War I goblets of his grandmother's. "This is him."

They held the photograph gently between them. A black and white image of a seemingly carefree marine smiled out at them.

"We don't have a picture of George, either when he was young or old. I have no idea if it's him," Brea said. "Monsieur Etienne, do you mind if I take a picture of this?" With his consent, she snapped a photo.

She quickly sent the image to Martha's daughter Susan. "Is this your grandfather George Harrison? Can you tell?" she texted.

Noah handed the photo back to their host. "What happened next?"

"As you can tell, our town is close to where much fighting occurred. It was a dangerous and scary time. A small group of Germans had taken up position at the edge of town, but thankfully when the Allied forces got near, they took off. It was like the Germans were there one day and gone the next, my father used to say.

"A day or two after they evacuated is when my father saw the American marine. He and a few of his fellow soldiers wandered into town, like I said, searching for food. My father and his five-year-old sister Cecile were outside with a large group of children when the soldiers walked past. With the Germans gone, their parents had finally allowed them to play out of doors again. The children followed the soldiers out of curiosity. The Americans smiled and tried to speak French with the children which made them laugh because their pronunciation was so awful.

"When the children grew tired of pestering the men, they returned to their play." He paused in his story to shake his head. "You must remember the children had been stuck indoors for a long time. It was like being released from quarantine or a long, drawn-out punishment. They did not think what they were doing. They were simply glad to be free to move about and explore."

"What did they do?"

"They ventured into the abandoned German position. I guess it looked like a fun hideout to them, like a playhouse or something. And they were curious having been cooped up for so long."

"What happened?" Brea and Noah were on the edge of their seats.

"The children found a large stash of items the Germans left behind—knapsacks, canned food, even old socks with holes in the toes. My father and several of his buddies discovered various canisters which they began to play with, standing them up, building a fort, doing whatever children do. Little Cecile had just discovered a box of tools when they heard shouting from outside.

"They stopped what they were doing long enough to locate the source of the commotion. Outside, one of the American soldiers was running at them and yelling. They did not understand his words, but they could tell he was upset. You understand they were used to soldiers being angry. But since they had been told they need not fear the Americans, they ignored the marine and went back to their play.

"But the soldier did not give up. While continuing to yell, he charged toward them. They froze, confused. As he drew nearer, he pointed his weapon at them, motioning for them to get out of the German bunker. At this, they finally scattered in fear." Alexandre shuddered. "I heard the story told so often that I can picture the events in my mind as if I were there.

"A few of the children ran home, but my father and many of his friends hid behind nearby buildings where the soldier had chased them. Peeking out to see what would happen next, my father realized he'd lost Cecile. She was nowhere to be seen.

"Scanning the path he'd taken, he saw the marine race back into the German fortifications. He emerged a few minutes later holding Cecile over his shoulder like a sack of potatoes. He ran with her away from the bunker. My father screamed, afraid of what this stranger might do with his sister.

"Without thinking, he ran toward them, but the soldier yelled at him and waved him off with the rifle he held in his free hand. My father stopped, not knowing what to do. As he watched, the marine gently placed Cecile on the ground. But before my father could even exhale, the soldier yanked something out of Cecile's hands which made her cry.

"With the idea of coming to her rescue, my father ran at the soldier with fists ready. But the man dashed off before my father could reach him. So, he yelled, '*Lâche!*' at the American, which means 'coward.' His friends behind him took up the chant, '*Lâche! Lâche!*'"

"Where did the marine go?" Noah asked.

"What did he take from Cecile?" Brea and Noah were mesmerized by the tale.

"To answer your second question first, when my father scooped up his little sister, she was furious. She told her brother, 'I was going to hit the metal things with my hammer, but that man grabbed my arm and wouldn't let me. I want my hammer. It's mine. I found it.' She tried to squirm out of his arms to chase after the soldier.

"The marine, by this time, had run back to the bunker and ducked inside. When he emerged, he frantically called to his fellow soldiers. Once they joined him, they talked excitedly amongst themselves, periodically checking the interior of the abandoned German location.

"It didn't take long, however, for the parents to come. The children who ran off had gone to their mothers and fathers complaining about the rude American soldier. You know how it goes, when one parent has been alerted, they gather all the adults in the neighborhood. By the time those children returned, their parents were in tow along with virtually every other parent in town.

"While the adults talked to the group of soldiers, the children huddled together to watch what would unfold. My father was used to seeing his mother and father as the ones in charge, but he told me he knew things were different in this case. The soldiers were obviously in control. By the tone of their voices, it was clear they were barking out orders.

"After a very short conversation, the parents hurried back to their children, shooing them to go on home. All they needed to say was, '*Yperite, yperite!*'"

"What is *yperite*?"

Monsieur Etienne, with blazing eyes, responded, "The Germans in their haste to retreat left a small stockpile of artillery shells. They were marked with yellow. The Germans called it yellow cross. The French called it *yperite*." He stared intently at his two guests. "You know it as mustard gas."

Both Noah and Brea gasped. Noah said, "I don't know much about World War I, but I've heard of mustard gas. Doesn't it kill people?"

"It is a very dangerous poison. It can burn the eyes resulting in permanent damage, blister your skin, irritate the airways causing chronic bronchitis. There is no safe exposure to mustard gas. And to a child … I hate to think of it." Alexandre stopped in his narrative to wipe his eyes.

126

When he spoke again, his voice was cold. "If anyone inhaled enough of it, it could blister the throat and lungs and, yes, cause death, an unpleasant death. It's likely half the town's children were there that day. My father told me in confidence that Cecile being so young never knew the extreme danger she had been in nor how she had put the marine at such risk."

The sobering situation silenced them for several moments.

"Did anyone in Viborgne die from it?" Noah timidly asked.

"No. It was close, but no. For the next several hours, the town watched from nearby as the Americans came. My father's family gathered at an aunt's house so they could see what was happening. Most of the town did the same—huddled in doorways, around windows, even sheltering in the nearby church to watch and pray.

"The Americans came with trucks and what seemed like a whole unit of soldiers. One by one, they carted off the shells, very carefully loading them into their trucks and taking them away. My father later heard they would likely use them against the Germans themselves. He told me that maybe he should have had more sympathy for the German soldiers, but he did not. It was deep into the evening before they were done. In the headlamps of a jeep, the soldier who originally chased off the children waved to the townspeople, giving them an all-clear signal.

"Before the parents could stop them, the children rushed outside to surround the soldier who had frightened them just a short time before. He crouched down as they smothered him with hugs and kisses. You can only imagine how grateful Viborgne was for saving their town but especially for saving their children."

Brea reached over and squeezed Noah's hand, but no one broke the heavy, reverent silence that engulfed the trio.

THE SCARF

"The Hero of Viborgne," Brea whispered to no one in particular. It was a different story than the one she had expected yet so much more powerful. "It's hard to overstate his impact."

Noah leaned his head on her shoulder. "Thanks for letting us come here, Mom."

"You're welcome. And thank you, Monsieur Etienne, for sharing your story."

"I am happy to share it. Not enough people have respect for something that happened over a hundred years ago. They don't understand its impact, as you pointed out. But you can understand why my father insisted I learn English. The events of that day were seared into his mind. He was grateful for that American until his dying day."

Brea's phone pinged with a text. "Hey, it's Susan. She got the picture I sent, but she's not sure if it's George. She says, 'Don't know about that one, but I went digging through old albums. I'm sending you a picture of my grandfather from World War I. See what you think.'"

The three of them gathered around Brea's phone waiting for the photo to load. Alexandre retrieved his picture of the American. When the image from Susan finished downloading, they stared at the screen and then Alexandre's photo, comparing the two.

Noah slumped back in his seat. "I can't tell. They're both skinny. They're both wearing a uniform—which is sooo helpful," he said while shaking his head.

"Hmm. They could be the same. The shape of the bodies is the same. The noses look similar, but the shadow across this face makes it hard to compare with the other one."

All of a sudden, M. Etienne burst out, "*Ça alors! C'est pas possible!*"

"What?"

He was shaking his head. "I can't believe it. He is the man. That's him!"

"How can you tell?" Noah was fully alert once again.

"The scarf." Alexandre was excitedly pointing at the picture on Brea's phone. Neither she nor Noah had noticed before, but the man in the picture was wearing a very non-military-issue scarf. It was haphazardly tied around his arm. Brea and Noah stared up to their grinning host, eager for an explanation.

"It seems I need to tell you a little more of my family history, and then you will understand. I have heard the story of the scarf since I was little. It mostly came from my aunts, so I never knew if the story was true. I figured it was one of those, what do you call it, wisps of imagination that grows bigger and bigger over time."

He got up and rummaged around in a nearby cupboard, finally extracting a framed photograph. "This is my father's family." He handed the picture to them while he pointed out family members. "This picture was taken after the war ended, a year after they met the American. These are my grandparents. They had six children. The oldest was Anne. She was born in 1902. Guillaume followed two years later. Then Denis was born in 1906 and Gabriel in 1908. This one is my father, Nicolas. He was, as you know already, born in 1910. Last came Cecile. She was born in 1913. The story of the scarf involved my father's two sisters.

"As my aunts told the story, the whole town was grateful to the American soldier who saved them. But Anne, who was 16 at the time, was quite taken by him. According to both her and Cecile, he was quite handsome. Anne owned a beloved scarf, which was a rare thing in the middle of the war. She offered her scarf to the American marine as a token of her thanks, or more likely, a token of her love.

"According to Tante Anne's telling of the story, the soldier accepted the scarf, smiled, and winked at her. But little Cecile was jealous and stamped her foot, saying, 'I wanted to give him a scarf so he'd be *my* boyfriend.' The object of their affection did not speak French, but one of his fellow soldiers did. He whispered in his ear what was being said. So, the marine bent down to Cecile's level and, speaking through his friend, said, 'I was just going to ask if you would tie it around my arm. Everyone will be so jealous and know that I'm taken.' Cecile, of course, immediately tied it around his arm.

"In your picture, look. The scarf is around his arm, and it is not neat and straight. It is messy and appears clumsy, as if a five-year-old tied it on." Alexandre laughed. "So, even that part of the story must be true. My sisters argued for years over what the soldier meant by 'I'm taken.' They agreed he was talking about them, but which one of them was he referring to? To whom did he belong?

"Only when my aunt Anne was getting married six years later did she tell Cecile that the American must have meant the younger sister after all. Cecile was 11 at the time. I believe it was her proudest moment."

"Wow," said Noah, "It really is him. I can't believe we found his story. You're probably the one person who could have helped us. Excuse me a minute." Noah ducked out of the house, retrieving something from the rental car.

"Monsieur Etienne, this is all we knew until now." He had put Martha's box in their car that morning. Now he flipped it upside down and showed it to their host. "It wasn't much to go on. But now we know everything. We know the whole story!"

"And who knew that a scarf would be the key to the whole thing," Brea said. But she noticed a cloud pass over Alexandre's face. "What's wrong?"

"The whole story? I am not so sure." He shook his head. "You must forgive an old man. I am 81, and not as agile of mind as I used to be. There is something I have forgotten—an important piece, but I do not recall what it is."

He stroked his chin, thinking. "I have not told this story in a long time, since no one is around to listen to it. The detail of the scarf is something I had not thought of for a long time. It has triggered a memory that I cannot quite explain or place. When my aunts talked of the scarf, everyone would immediately start retelling the story of the Hero of Viborgne, but the thing that troubles me is the memory of my father. He would disagree with them about something. I know he revered the American marine, but there was a part of the story he claimed everyone left out. Only, I do not remember what it was."

. . .

After Alexandre Etienne profusely apologized for his faulty memory, he assured Brea and Noah he would contact them when he remembered. He'd first said, "if he remembered," but then caught himself and tried to cover his tracks. They wrote down the name of their hotel and its phone number, hoping for the best while trying not to fear the worst.

"What we did learn was pretty cool. George Harrison was an amazing hero," Noah said on their drive back. "I would have been completely satisfied if Monsieur Etienne hadn't said he was missing something. It's frustrating to be so close but still know there's a hole."

"I know. Part of me wishes he'd kept his lost secrets lost. Then we wouldn't be wondering about them. But still, when I think about what could have happened if George Harrison hadn't been paying attention … wow."

"Yeah, wow."

HAZEL

While opening the door of their hotel room, Brea got a text from her dad. "Are you up for a video call?"

She dropped her things so she could immediately respond. "Yes, and perfect timing. We have stories to tell."

"So do we!"

"Noah, hurry and turn on my computer. I think your grandpa and grandma learned something."

Earl Roberts insisted they tell their story first. Impatient though Brea and Noah were, they found themselves caught up in the events that transpired a century earlier. When they finished, both Earl and Lizzie were speechless. As if they had agreed ahead of time, neither Brea nor Noah mentioned the missing information.

"We didn't expect to find an eyewitness to tell us about the Hero of Viborgne, or technically a second-hand witness, but it was incredible," Noah said.

"That's fantastic," Lizzie said. "You'll have to tell Martha's children about their grandfather. I'm sure they have no idea what he did."

"I hadn't thought about them wanting to know, but he is their relative," Noah said. His face fell ever so slightly, and Brea took note with the intention of asking him about it later. He quickly recovered and said, "So, what did you find? Is it about great-great-grandma's journal?"

"As a matter of fact, it is," Earl said. "I was reading through it. She was there!"

"There? Where exactly is 'there'?" Brea said.

"She was in Vicenza, at the U.S. base hospital."

"You're kidding! This story just got a lot more interesting." Noah pulled himself closer to the screen.

"If you're guessing where this is going, you're absolutely right. But let me lay out the details for you anyway. Hazel was a nurse during the war. She was assigned to the hospital in Vicenza. At first, she talks about helping set things up and then mentions the general care and condition of the soldiers being brought there. But pretty soon she starts talking more and more about one particular soldier. She didn't name him in the beginning. He's simply an Italian who ran messages for his commander, and she said while he was in France delivering a message, he was shot. He was cared for at a field hospital in France for a couple months, but an infection set in, so they sent him back to Italy to her hospital. Lizzie, where's that part I wanted to read to them?"

"Here it is, dear," she said after a few minutes of page turning.

"Go ahead and read it."

"Okay. Hazel writes:"

He is handsome, but I try not to pay attention to that. It is harder to ignore how charming he is. He speaks French with a realistic-sounding accent. It makes me do a double take whenever he uses French because I forget for a moment he is Italian. He alternates between that and the Italian. As far as communication, it makes no difference because he knows I don't understand either one. He does it because he knows it drives me crazy, and even though I try to hide it, he also knows I love how both languages sound. He is working on his English too. He said it came in handy in France with all those dumb Americans around. He says this with a wink, knowing it also drives me crazy.

"She doesn't mention him again for a week. But then she says much of the same thing."

My Italian patient (it's funny to call him that since we have so many Italian patients here) is continuing to get better. His infection is almost completely cleared up, and his wounds are healing nicely. He is always flirting, and his English is also improving. He calls me aside anytime I pass so he can practice his English, or so he says. If he wasn't so amiable, I'd probably refuse.

"She has a big gap in her entries, and then she writes:"

I have been so busy lately, but I had to write today. The war is ending! We're all so excited—and relieved. We have had very few deaths here at the hospital, but even one is too many. And I am weary of the illnesses and the injuries in men who should be in the prime of their lives. Beniamino (my Italian) is thankfully doing quite well. He has been healthy enough to be discharged from the hospital for the last two weeks, but he keeps finding excuses to stay—a blister on his thumb or a rash on his foot. He is not shirking his military duties because when he is released from here, he will also be discharged from his military service. He was shot twice, a bullet cutting through his right shin and another grazing the side of his head just above his left ear. The shot to his leg hit bone and soon after became infected. His head wound, on the other hand, was superficial. He has a scar line where the hair doesn't grow, but that's the extent of it. The irony of it is that a leg wound does not automatically disqualify him from military service and, had it not been for the scratch on his head, he would have been expected to report back to duty in the Italian army, regardless of the outcome of the war. But with so many injured soldiers, it appears from the notations in his record they decided to discharge him as soon as they saw the words: shot in the head. I probably shouldn't be taking such an interest in the details of a single patient. I can say nothing in my defense. I'll only add that I haven't been discouraging his delays in leaving the hospital. However, I know it's just putting off the inevitable. This has been a pleasant fling, one that can't last.

"That's where her entry ends."

"But clearly not where her story ends," Brea said.

"What's next?" Noah was interested in the story as much as the rest of them.

His grandfather grinned. "It sucks you in, doesn't it? Once I started reading, I called your grandma over. We've been reading over each other's shoulders for the last hour. We had to call you right away. Go on, Lizzie, read them the rest."

"Okay. So, we have to skip a few entries where she talks about the end of the war and what's going to happen. She mentions the hospital will be closed. Most of the staff will be returning to the United States soon. Some of the nurses plan to do a little sightseeing around Europe first. They invited her to join them, but she says she'd decided to stay behind until the very end at the hospital and help shut it down."

"She doesn't say it, but we all know why she stayed behind," Earl said with a wink.

"But where is Beniamino? He wouldn't still be in the hospital if they're shutting it down, would he?"

"You're right, Noah. Let me read this entry."

Beniamino was officially discharged from the army and from the hospital. His mother is angry he didn't return to Orvieto. Instead, he found a room to rent here in Vicenza. I am busy at the hospital, but he finds me at least once every day. I cannot help but blush when I see him or hear his voice. Now, whether he is speaking Italian, French, or English, I can tell it's him. My heart makes a leap and I find focusing on my work to be impossible. When I am with him, I have no worries. When I am alone in my bed at night, I fear it might be the Florence Nightingale effect, that he is simply attracted to me because I helped nurse him back to health. I am dreading leaving to go home.

"I have to skip ahead several entries to the important one. In between, she expresses much of the same sentiment as I just read you. In May of 1919, she writes:"

Since I have been back home, Beniamino and I have exchanged letters. The time it takes for them to arrive is agonizing, but he wrote one before I ever left so it was waiting for me when I arrived. It was the best one of all. He told me he had been holding back a surprise. He is coming! He is coming to America! Before I left Italy, he told me he loved me, and I told him I loved him too. But I thought that was the end of it, that we were saying goodbye to what could have been. I am partly angry at him for keeping his plans a secret, but I'm so ecstatic that it's impossible to stay upset with him.

"We haven't read any of her entries after that yet," Earl said, "We got this far and wanted to call you. But we already know they were married in April of 1920."

"What a sweet ending," Brea said, smiling. "We walked the streets of Vicenza. I thought we hadn't found much there, but we were walking the same streets they walked when they were falling in love. I know a lot changes in a hundred years, but it was still the same geography. That's amazing."

"Yes, it is," Lizzie said. "Did you take pictures?"

"We take pictures everywhere," Noah said as he rolled his eyes.

Brea had to laugh. "He loses it every time I say, 'But wait, we need a picture.'" She knew he didn't actually mind. It was the playful banter that had returned to their relationship after being absent for far too long.

After catching up on the happenings at home and the events in Europe, they ended their call. Closing her laptop, Brea turned to Noah. "That was great. That answered our questions and then some. I'm so glad Hazel wrote her story down."

"Me too. It didn't change anything, not really, not for them. But it's important to me. It's nice to know what happened."

"With all your writing, don't forget to write your own story. You never know when it might mean something—to you or to someone else."

"I guess you're right. You can too, you know, write your story."

Brea gave him an uneven smile. "I guess I asked for that. I'll try, okay." He pretended to look offended but didn't pull it off very well. The change in his face triggered Brea's memory. "Tell me something, Noah. What's up with George Harrison's story?"

Noah knit his brow in confusion. "George's story? Nothing's up with it other than there's a hole in it."

"Is that what you were thinking about? Your grandma mentioned telling Martha's children about it. I was watching your face. Something's wrong. Was that it?"

He paused before responding. "Not really. The hole wasn't the problem. I was thinking … don't be mad at me, but I was thinking that George is kind of mine. It's become personal to me. I mean, geez, we took this trip to figure out George and the whole Hero of Viborgne business. Sharing what we learned with Grandma and Grandpa is one thing, but Mimi's family is something else. George actually belongs to them. If I tell them his story, it's like I'll be giving it to them to keep and own. It won't belong to me anymore. I won't have any claim on it." He shrugged. "It doesn't make a lot of sense, but that's how I feel. It's selfish, I know, but … well, I'm not ready to stop being selfish about it."

"Okay, first off, thanks for telling me and not shying away from my question. I appreciate your honesty. And second, I understand and I don't think you're being selfish. I know you. If your grandma hadn't said anything, you would have thought of it yourself. You would be the first to suggest telling all of Martha's family about George. Think about it. We've already been keeping Susan in the loop. Just because he's their blood relative doesn't mean you don't have a connection with him too. The one doesn't cancel the other out."

Noah beamed. "Thanks, Mom. I hadn't thought of it that way. And we have learned about Beniamino too. He's my blood relative. I can claim him."

"Noah, they're all part of your story. Your great-great-grandfather made your physical life possible, but Martha made that life better. She wouldn't have existed without George existing. And George's story inspires us. I don't know about you, but it makes me want to look around and take care of others. Those children would all have died or suffered needlessly if he hadn't done what he did. He's a hero to me, not just to Viborgne."

"Okay. I can live with that. So, what now?"

"In what way?"

"Well, all we can do now about George is hope Monsieur Etienne remembers what he's forgotten. I think it's clear we're not going to find that information anywhere else."

"No. We wouldn't know the things we already do without him. And he's trying to remember something his father claimed everyone else left out. So,

Alexandre is likely the one person on the planet who has that information. It's great that we connected with him, but I'm not too hopeful about him remembering."

"Same. So, what now, Mom? Do we hang around hoping he'll come up with it? Should we go on to something else? We didn't really have any plans after Château-Thierry, but I don't want to go home yet."

"I'm not ready to go home either. So, I'm glad we agree on that. We're not that far from Paris. We could head that way. I'm sure there are lots of other options. Other than this little area, we haven't seen what France has to offer. And now," she said, winking, "we have a French-English dictionary." Noah shook his head in response. "But, seriously, why don't we stay put and take a break for a day. We can relax, go to the pool. It will give us a chance to research what else we might want to see. You can help me do our laundry. And we'll use those things as an excuse to wait on Monsieur Etienne."

"That's as good a plan as any. What time is it? I'm starving."

Brea laughed. "Why don't you get cleaned up and we'll go to dinner."

"I'll be ready before you know it," Noah said as he popped into the bathroom.

She beamed at her son. This trip had been such a godsend.

Her eyes fell on Martha's box that Noah had brought back in from the car. She knew the next envelope was for her.

Before she could change her mind, she opened the box. The envelopes were slightly askew from Noah upending the box in front of Alexandre, but envelope #6 was easy enough to locate. She tore it open quickly, wanting to view it in private before Noah finished in the bathroom.

Share with Noah what you've written and why. That was it. What in the world was Martha talking about? Brea picked up the discarded envelope to double check who it was for. It said Brea clearly across the front. Of course, the note itself made it clear she was to share with Noah and not the other way around. Still, it didn't make sense. This note was so similar to Noah's notes— both so far about sharing his writing with her.

Befuddled, Brea returned the note to its envelope and placed the envelope back into the box. "She must have been confused. She mixed us up somehow," she mumbled to herself.

"What, Mom?" Noah had emerged without her notice. "Who are you talking about?"

"Oh, nothing. Martha just … I don't know. I think her age finally took a toll." She shook her head. "Are you ready for dinner?"

"Of course." Noah grinned.

ENVELOPE #6

Brea woke up early and quietly sorted their laundry to take to a local laundromat once Noah got up. When he still hadn't stirred, she opened her laptop to catch up on work emails once again. She was halfway through responding to the first email when it hit her. "I write code!"

She turned around to see if her outburst had roused the sleeping teen. She was disappointed it had not.

Brea finished dealing with her emails, did internet searches on the best things to do in Paris and the surrounding areas, and ordered room service breakfast for Noah and herself. By the time he awoke, she had finished her portion of the breakfast and was well into a new e-book, the envelope from Martha once again forgotten.

"What do you want to do with your day?" Brea said when Noah stretched and started to nibble on breakfast.

"Honestly, I want to race back to Viborgne to hear the rest of Monsieur Etienne's story, but I guess I'll settle for walking around town and buying souvenirs. Did you have anything in mind?"

"Nope. We could look for more cheeses to try?" she said with a playful smirk.

"Oh, sure, and make me try them first. I don't think so."

Brea laughed. "I'll try them first, okay?"

"Okay." Noah seemed satisfied.

"But remember, I liked the bleu cheese." She had a wicked glint in her eye.

"And you were worried about me going off the deep end. It's too bad Mimi isn't here to set you straight. I could trust that woman. You … I'm beginning to wonder."

"Martha! I forgot. Noah, I opened the next envelope, and I figured out what it means!"

Noah tilted his head and considered his mom. "What do you mean, you figured it out? I thought her instructions have always been pretty clear."

"Your instructions, maybe. But mine have been different—like watch Noah's face. Okay, bad example. That sounds simple, but it took me a bit to figure out how that was different from what I was already doing. So, this one said: *Share with Noah what you've written and why.*"

He lifted his eyebrows. "Mom, that's almost exactly like my notes that you just agreed were easy to understand."

"Okay. I know it sounds that way on the surface, but think about it, Noah. I don't write things like you do."

He was about to respond when he stopped with his mouth open. "Oh. You're right. So, what *does* that mean?"

"I didn't know. I opened it last night, and I thought for sure Martha had made a mistake. But this morning, I figured it out. I'm a programmer. I write code!"

"Hmm. That's interesting. But I don't think I'll understand any of it, even if you do show it to me."

"Of course not." Brea was taking a turn to roll her eyes at him. "It's about what the code does, and there's the part about why I do it."

"Okay. That makes sense. So, what are you coding, and why do you do it?" He pulled his feet up onto the bed, sitting cross-legged, like he was ready to hear a boring lecture.

"It's not that bad. Get dressed, and let's take all these dirty clothes to the car. I'll tell you while we're doing our laundry. That should still leave us plenty of time for wandering and shopping."

. . .

Once their clothes were busily agitating in the washers, Brea and Noah settled into two hard chairs to wait. "Okay, Mom. I'm ready."

"Comfortable?"

"No, but go ahead. I'm listening."

Brea chuckled. "Fair enough. So, your dad left us in solid financial shape. That gave me time to think through what I wanted to do. I studied computer science in college with the idea of writing educational software for children. After weighing my options, that's the plan I went back to. Only, I didn't have to work for someone else. With the fallback of money in the bank, I started doing freelance work. It took a bit to get steady clients, but they came in time.

"My whole idea was to work enough to continue to pad our bank account but not so much that I couldn't devote a lot of time to you. To that end, I worked sparsely when you were a toddler. Once you went to school, I worked more hours—your school hours. I figured with only one parent, you needed as much stability as I could give you."

"I didn't know that. Why didn't you tell me this before?"

"I have no idea. I guess I assumed you already knew. A poor assumption on my part. I've been a freelance programmer so long that I took for granted what I do and that you knew all about it. But I don't talk about it, so that logic was rather faulty."

"You think?"

Brea tried to give him a dirty look, but they both started laughing.

"Honestly, I've intentionally worked hard to compartmentalize my work. I code when you're at school so I can be available when you're home. During the summer when you don't have school, I try to work in the early mornings. I didn't realize I had compartmentalized so completely."

"I obviously knew you wrote code, but I never thought about what it was. It's like you just sent it off into the cloud, and ..." He grimaced. "Now that I say it, it sounds pretty lame. So, what kind of educational software do you write?"

"I like to create math games—for all ages really. I've taken games I've written for third graders, slapped a different label on them, and marketed them to adults. Both have done well. I used to make them for various websites, but then we switched over to apps, and abandoned the PC-based approach."

"What do you mean by 'we'?"

"Geez. I can't believe I haven't told you all this. I have four other people I team up with on a regular basis. One guy is great with the graphics. He handles the final release, making sure things are visually appealing and clean. The rest of us take on whatever role is needed at the time. They're covering for me while we're here on this trip. I've covered for them plenty, so they don't mind. They just know I usually only work during school hours."

"What do your apps look like?"

"I really haven't shown you?" When Noah shook his head, Brea opened her phone and showed him various apps she helped create.

"I know these. You let me play them all the time when I was little. But I didn't realize you made them."

"Well, I have to plead the fifth on that one. I thought you might not like playing them if you knew your mom made them. You might not take them seriously. And I have one other confession." She winced before continuing. "You were kind of my guinea pig. The nice title is beta tester. I often gave you a prototype to see what worked and what didn't or to see if you liked it or not. Usually that went well. But one game you hated, so we scrapped the whole thing. Another game, you found a loophole and beat the entire thing in one afternoon. When we eventually released that one, it was radically different from where it started."

"I suppose I forgive you for that. But we might have to discuss some back pay issues."

"Oh, is that how this is going? I'd be willing to discuss that if we also discuss cooking, cleaning, and chauffeur services provided to you, previously free of charge, for thirteen years now. Back pay works both ways, you know."

"Okay, okay, you win." Noah laughed. "But you were supposed to tell me why you wrote these. Is there another reason?"

"Nice change of subject there. Yeah, I guess there is. I liked the ability to work from home and basically be a stay-at-home mom most of the time. But that's more about the logistics of the job, not the job itself. The reason I coded what I did was to help children. I insisted early on that we find a way to provide access to our games and apps to poorer and at-risk kids. I wanted to make a difference in their lives."

"Do you still feel that way?"

"What do you mean?"

"Do you still want to make a difference? You talked in past tense."

"I did, didn't I? When it comes down to it, I haven't been as engaged lately in what I do."

"Why?"

She studied Noah. How honest should she be? "I've been distracted. I've been worried about you, and I couldn't focus. So, lately I've been working in more of a clean-up role, tightening up the code rather than being the originator of it or coming up with the ideas."

"I'm sorry, I guess."

She shrugged. "It's part of being a mom." She bumped his arm with hers. "Of course, it's better not having a reason to worry. But I think we've been making progress on that."

"Yeah, I think so."

The laundry interrupted the moment. It was time to move the wet clothes to the dryers. By the time they'd paid for the loads and settled back down, Brea figured the moment had passed. She was wrong.

"Tell me what you're working on now? Are you tweaking older apps or do you have new ones coming up?"

"You really want to know?"

"Yes. It's actually interesting. I think it's cool what you do."

"Okay." Brea had a hard time containing her smile. "I haven't been creating new apps lately, but I do have ideas I've been keeping on the back burner." She pulled a small notepad out of her purse and sketched out her latest ideas for Noah.

Before long, they were both engrossed in the project, each pitching in ideas of what could work to either enhance the educational aspect or the gaming experience. When they stopped to take a break, they realized their dryers had long since finished.

Brea gathered up the notes while Noah retrieved their clothes from the dryers. "Thanks, Noah."

"For what?"

"For the great ideas. For encouraging me. I thought my work was taking me away from you. Who knew the opposite could be just as true?"

"I guess you're welcome then."

"I mean it, Noah. It's like you've given me back a piece of myself."

"You want to help people. I think that's great." He shrugged. "But you can't share a water bottle that's empty."

Brea stared at him for a moment. Then she turned to carry their clothes to the car. Over her shoulder, she said, "You should write that one down."

Noah grinned. "Already planning on it."

. . .

The main goal for shopping the rest of the day was to keep their minds off Alexandre Etienne and the fact that he hadn't called them. Fortunately, for their peace of mind if not their pocketbook, they found many unique souvenirs to add to their growing stash.

After dropping off their purchases and enjoying a delicious meal at the hotel restaurant, Brea and Noah made their way to the patio. It was a relatively quiet night with only the muffled laughter of other guests wafting over from the open restaurant windows.

"This is a beautiful night," Brea said. She was gazing up at the sky where a few stars were starting to appear.

"Thanks for telling me about your work today, Mom."

Brea turned at the serious note in his voice. "Sure, Noah. I'm just sorry I hadn't told you sooner."

Noah let out a sigh. "Mom, I want to tell you stuff, but not every detail. Since it's only the two of us, you already know so much about me. You're involved in almost every aspect of my life. I need friends and activities that are just mine."

"I get that. And I agree with you for the most part. But what about the party—the drinking, the drugs? I didn't know about that. It could have ended up so much worse."

"Yeah, I know. I've been thinking about that. I think I have a compromise."

"I'm listening."

"Sundays. We reserve Sunday evenings for the two of us. I'll talk to you about what's going on in my life. You don't need to hound me for information during the week because on Sunday I'll tell you. I won't tell you everything, but I'll tell you enough."

Brea nodded. "Okay. You've made good decisions before. So, I'll trust you. But, Noah?"

"Yeah?" He was wary about what was coming next.

"What about in the moment? Some things can't wait until the weekend."

"Can you just trust me to tell you?"

"Can I? I want to. You have to remember Martha gave me your tell. I'm more aware of your face than I used to be. What do you want me to do when I see that look on your face that says something's not right? I want to respect your space, Noah. I really do. So, help me know what to do in those cases. I don't want to repeat what happened."

"With the party or with Dad?"

Brea stared out at the landscape beyond the patio, unable to respond for a time. Finally, in a subdued voice, she said, "The party's easier to address. Use me as an excuse to get out of uncomfortable situations, if you want."

"I did. I told Riley you'd kill me if you found out. I'm not sure it helped."

"Then say you have to take your mom to her AA meeting or pick her up from the tattoo parlor."

Noah laughed. "Okay, I get the point. I guess I can be more creative if I need to be. Hopefully, I'll get better at avoiding those situations in the first place."

"That's a better solution to be sure."

"But what about Dad?"

"That's a lot harder to deal with." Brea's voice came as if from far away, deep in the recesses of her mind. "I thought I could trust him. I thought I knew everything about him."

She grew quiet. Noah knew enough to wait for her to speak, but he leaned in, encouraging her to continue.

Her voice was almost a whisper. "You're starting to look like him, you know. When I see you, it's often startling, as if you're a younger version of Paul—back before he made decisions that steered his life off course. You've got the same wavy, auburn hair, the cheekbones, the arched eyebrows—but it's your eyes, Noah. Your eyes have the same intensity his did—sometimes in a mischievous twinkle or a studious stare or even filled with great joy. I know Martha has got me watching your face, but she would never have needed to tell me to pay attention to your eyes. I can't avoid noticing them. You know the saying, 'The apple doesn't fall far from the tree.' It's hard to let go of that." She studied Noah, and the strength in her voice returned. "But I'll try. I do trust you, Noah. I have to live life like I can trust you."

Noah held her gaze. "Then I'll try to deserve that trust."

"I'm not expecting perfection. That's not reasonable. But I think we've learned when there are problems, it's easier to address them together."

"Agreed. But, Mom, this is a two-way street. You have to promise to tell me stuff too. Tell me what you're working on, what you care about. And, Mom," he paused to make sure he had her full attention, "tell me if you're scared. That's so much better than you trying to smother me instead."

"Okay. It's a deal."

"You know the whole apple thing … well, if you're worried about me, can you tell me it reminds you of Dad instead of assuming I'm acting like him, the bad side of him, I mean?"

"Okay. I'll try to do that, and I'll try to do it without interfering too much in your life. I'm not promising I'll be perfect at it though."

Noah tipped his head. "I think someone told me they didn't expect me to be perfect. So that's a two-way street too."

Brea winced. "I know I said that, but I think I got it backwards. A few days ago, I gave you mom lecture #27 about not putting so much pressure on yourself to be the perfect kid. I guess while we're giving each other a break, we need to remember to give ourselves that same break."

"Yeah. How did you ever make it to 40 anyway? This life stuff is hard."

Brea turned on him but saw the glint in his eye. "I'm 36, for the record. If you want to make it to that age, you'd best keep that tidbit in mind."

"Are you saying I need to always remember you're 36, like in ten years, I should still think you're 36?"

"Not what I meant, but yes, I do believe that will work."

"So, what's next, Mom?"

"That's a bit of a loaded question. Do you think we're good here? Have we made progress?"

"I hope so. Time will tell, won't it?"

"Yes, like you said, the whole apple thing …"

Noah smiled and his eyes flashed with intensity. "Mom, why don't you say that?"

"Say what?"

"When you're worried about me, remind me of 'the whole apple thing.' No long, drawn-out lecture, just 'the whole apple thing.'"

"I could do that. And if I'm starting to be overprotective and smother you, or if I'm not telling you enough … you remind me of the same thing."

"I can do that too."

"So, back to your earlier question, 'What now?'—in strictly logistical terms. What should we do tomorrow? I've looked up different options around here. We could head to Paris or the French Riviera. But I think I may have found a better option. I'm guessing you're like me and don't want to leave here yet—you know, in case M. Etienne remembers something." Noah nodded. "Well, if that's the case, about forty minutes from here is Disneyland Paris. What do you think?"

"What do I think? I think you're brilliant!"

Brea chuckled. "Then we probably better head to bed. I'm guessing we'll want to get an early start and be there when it opens."

"When does it open?"

"At 7:30 in the morning."

"Then what are we waiting for? Let's get to bed."

DISNEYLAND PARIS

Disneyland Paris is actually two parks—Disneyland Park and Walt Disney Studios Park. While they waited in line to buy tickets, they used their French-English dictionary to ask those around them for advice. The general consensus was that you could buy a one-day ticket, but you wouldn't be able to fit everything in if you did, so you were better off paying for a two or three-day pass. At least they thought that's what people were telling them. It seemed like a safe assumption.

Without any clear, future plans, they decided to go for it. Brea contacted their hotel to extend their reservation. That was simple enough. And with a handy credit card, the three-day pass was simple enough as well.

They took turns throughout the day picking the next ride or activity to try. Their day ranged from the Mad Hatter's Tea Cups, which they chose to ride multiple times to see how fast they could get themselves spinning, to the roller coaster type rides of Indiana Jones and the Temple of Peril and Big Thunder Mountain.

To Noah's surprise, everything made his mom laugh. "I'd pegged you for a screamer on roller coasters, to be honest, Mom."

Brea tousled his hair. "I guess you don't know me that well. The bigger the thrill ride, the more it makes me laugh—at least when I know it's well controlled, unlike a certain luge ride down a mountain. Then again, maybe I'm just covering up my terror, who knows?" And then she laughed some more.

Noah shrugged. "You're a mother of mystery. I wasn't sure how much fun Disneyland would be with my mom, but as long as you don't ever tell my friends … I'm having a blast!"

They stayed late, squeezing every ounce of fun out of their time. "I'm glad we got the multi-day pass. There's a ton we haven't seen yet," Noah said, examining a park map in the car with the flashlight from his phone. "We haven't even gone to the Walt Disney Studios Park yet. We'll have to hit that first tomorrow."

. . .

They approached their second day differently than they had the first. Over a rushed breakfast that morning at the hotel, they'd spread the park map between them, circling in green attractions they didn't want to miss, those with potential in yellow, and some they wanted to revisit in orange. Then they planned out a logical order of attack. When they got to the park, Noah became their navigator with Brea working hard to keep up.

By the time evening approached, they had ridden or visited everything in green. They enjoyed each attraction, but Noah was particularly pleased that he got his mother to scream on The Twilight Zone Tower of Terror. He wasn't going to let her live it down either, and much to her chagrin, they'd opted to get a photo taken of themselves during the ride. Noah had proof to back up his claims.

"What a great day. I'm not sure you can get me to ride that *thing* again," Brea said, without needing to explain which *thing* she was referring to, "but I really enjoyed everything. Hanging out with you was pretty fun."

"I agree. Again, just don't tell anyone."

"Now, that's not fair. You know I'm going to tell Amy all about it when we get home. I mean, seriously, child. It's as if you don't even know me."

Noah laughed. "Sure. You can tell Amy as long as I get to tell her about your screams."

"You drive a hard bargain. I'm not sure I like such blackmail—and from my own son!"

Noah grinned. "Thanks, Mom."

"For the fact that I screamed or for the permission to tell Amy—which I haven't given yet, by the way."

"For the trip. The last two days have been really fun. But the whole thing has been great."

"You're welcome. And I agree with you. I hadn't realized what an awesome kid you are. Do you think we can do this back home? Here we're stuck together. We need each other—maybe because you're the only person speaking a language I can understand, but still … So, do you think we can still work together when we get home?"

"I think so. I want to. Maybe that's enough—to want to."

"I hope you're right. Martha said to have an adventure together. Life is a pretty big adventure. What do you say? We at least try to do it together? For the next few years anyway. At some point, I get to kick the baby bird out of the nest. But in the meantime, I hope I can teach you how to fly."

"If you're willing to try that *thing*, then I suppose I can go along for the rest." He grinned at his mom. "Oh, and by the way, Matteo and Carlo love the picture of you screaming," he said before quickly dodging out of range of her elbow.

. . .

Walking into the hotel that night, Brea was surprised to be summoned to the front desk. "You have a message, Ms. Cass."

"I do? Who would leave me a message?"

Noah nudged his mom. "Monsieur Etienne."

"You're right. I'd almost forgotten. Do you think …?" She hardly dared hope, knowing getting all the answers in life is a rare thing. Beside her, Noah crossed his fingers.

The front desk clerk handed her a written message. It was from Alexandre, no last name, as if he were their oldest and dearest friend. Brea grinned widely and tilted the note so Noah could read over her shoulder. It read: "I have it! Can you come tomorrow at 10?"

Noah let out a holler with a fist pump, startling the clerk and the two other guests in the lobby. "Sorry," he said sheepishly.

When they were alone in their room, Brea said, "So, what do you want to do about it?"

"What do you mean?"

"We have tickets for one more day at Disney. I can call M. Etienne in the morning. I'm sure we could meet with him the following day."

"Are you kidding? Disney has been fun, but if you don't mind losing the cost of the day, I'd just as soon go solve our mystery. That's what we came here for." But then he was quick to add, "Unless you'd rather get one more day in at Disneyland."

"It has been fun. But I'm completely fine blowing it off. I agree. This is why we came—to find answers. But I wanted to make sure you felt the same way I did."

They figured it was too late at night to confirm the time with M. Etienne, but they planned to call him first thing in the morning.

As they were drifting off to sleep, a sleepy-voiced Noah said, "I figured we weren't going to hear from him. And I decided I was okay with that. Everything was good. But I was wrong. This is so much better."

THE JOURNAL ENTRY

Brea and Noah sat eagerly in Alexandre Etienne's study. He insisted on preparing them coffee or tea before they got started. If they could have figured out a polite way to decline, they would have. Instead, they both opted for tea and sat fidgeting, knowing they wouldn't be able to drink a drop until they heard what M. Etienne had to tell them.

While he was busying himself, Brea whispered to Noah, "He reminds me of Martha."

"Mimi? How?"

"He's old fashioned. You can't have guests without giving them food."

"Oh, I figured that was Mimi's way of softening us up to talk. But it is a hospitality kind of thing, isn't it?"

"Yes. It also worked to keep us around longer. You couldn't leave until you finished Martha's muffin or cookie or whatever."

"That's true. It must be lonely to be old." He said it casually, but once he did, the two of them exchanged a glance. This man must be very lonely.

"Didn't he say something about not sharing this story for a long time because there was no one to listen to it? I'll bet he doesn't get visitors often."

"Yeah. Probably not."

When Alexandre emerged with tea and croissants, Brea and Noah weren't as impatient as they had been only moments before. "I noticed, Monsieur Etienne," Brea said, "that you have a beautiful garden out front of your house. Do you take care of it all by yourself?"

He set down the refreshments and smiled wistfully. "That would have been my dear Amélie. She was the natural gardener. I think you call it having a green thumb. I take care of it myself now that she's gone, but it was her garden. It's pretty now, but it was magnificent when she was in charge."

"Was she your wife?" Noah asked.

"Yes. We were married for forty-seven years. We never had children, so her flowers became her children. How could I not keep caring for them?"

"That's so sweet. How long ago did she pass away?"

"Seven years ago." He choked up and turned his head while wiping away a tear.

"I lost my husband twelve years ago. You get past it, but I'm not sure you get over it."

He smiled at Brea, the lines around his eyes sparkling with his remaining tears. "Thank you."

"Do you have a picture of her?" Noah said.

"Yes," Alexandre said, brightening considerably. "She was a beautiful woman." With a spryness that belied his age, he hopped up from his chair and quickly retrieved a framed portrait and a photo album.

At their urging, he told them stories of his wife and their lives together. They continued to pepper him with questions—charmed by his tender remembrances.

As midday drew near, Monsieur Etienne insisted they join him for lunch. After hanging up from ordering a lunch to be delivered, he stopped in his tracks. "Wait! This is not why you came. I have stories to tell you, and not about my wife."

Both Brea and Noah were surprised that he was the one to remember the whole point of their visit. "I honestly forgot," Noah said.

"Yes," Alexandre laughed, "that was my problem. And despite racking my brain, I couldn't bring to mind what I'd forgotten."

"So, when did you finally remember?"

"I didn't."

Noah and Brea stared at each other in alarm. "I thought you said …" Brea tentatively said.

Alexandre chuckled to himself. "Sorry to do that to you. I never could recall that missing piece, but I finally remembered that my father, Nicolas, wrote it down. Then it was simply a matter of finding his journals and pinpointing the right one. That's what took me a couple days."

"Wow! That's great." Noah was once again on the edge of his seat.

Alexandre reached over to a side table and picked up an old journal. He opened it at a bookmark. "His earlier journals were in French, but as soon as he could, he began to learn English. Then his entries are a mixture of French and English. Whenever he discussed the Hero of Viborgne, however, he wrote in English. I told you he always insisted there was more to the story, a part people often left out. This is it." He tapped the open page with his finger before beginning to read his father's entry.

I am just back from visiting my youngest sister, Cecile, and her family. We were reminiscing about our childhood. And, of course, The Hero came up. He always does. We wouldn't have had a childhood without him. But it struck me that she left part of the story out. When I volunteered the missing details, she laughed at me, claiming I had embellished the story over time. Since she was only five when it happened, I naturally assumed she'd forgotten. So, we called Anne and then Guillaume to compare tales. They did not recall the additional details either.

I know they occurred because I was at such an impressionable age that I was awed by what I heard. I can only assume the others, filled with gratitude for the young marine, tuned out anything that appeared to diminish his bravery. I, however, thought it enhanced it—because he insisted on telling the whole story.

I don't know if I wrote this down when I was young (I was a sporadic journal keeper), but I'm writing it here to ensure a record of it exists. I fear I am the only one to recall this.

The story of the Hero of Viborgne is well known—how at great personal risk he shooed the children away from the munitions the Germans left behind, even stopping Cecile from hitting a mustard-gas-filled shell with a hammer, and how he then alerted his superiors so the shells could be removed safely. The whole town was grateful to the American marine for saving all its children. I was certainly happy!

I was young enough that I couldn't remember a time without war. It had become part of life. And because it was part of life, we had grown used to death, even become callous to it. But when it is your own life that is threatened, it strikes you very differently.

I was in complete awe of the man. When I heard the town was going to throw a banquet to honor the marine, I could hardly wait. I insisted our family arrive early so we could sit close to the dais.

Alexandre paused his reading. "Here. My father tucked this picture in with the entry." He handed an old photograph over to Brea and Noah. It showed a portion of a large room filled with tables. The photo focused on the head table where a soldier was standing with an older gentleman, both smiling for the camera.

Brea turned the picture over. On the back was written: *Héros de Viborgne George Harrison et maire.*

"I'm sure you can understand the Hero of Viborgne and the name of your neighbor's father. He is standing with the mayor. *Et maire* means 'and mayor.'"

"I can't believe this. It's great! Mom, can you take a picture of this?"

After Brea snapped a picture with her phone of both the front and the back of the photo, she returned it to Monsieur Etienne. "What's significant about this dinner?"

"Ahh, yes. Let me keep reading."

I barely ate. I was watching his every move. He had needed to get permission from his sergeant to attend the banquet, but he and the fellow soldiers who had been with him were allowed to come to our celebration as the guests of honor.

After the meal, the mayor stood and praised the soldiers who came to our aid, but he reserved his highest praise for Private George Harrison who started everything in motion by noticing the town's children, recognizing their hazardous situation, and running into danger himself to protect them. I had not known his name before that moment. He was simply "The Marine" or "The Hero."

While the mayor went on and on, an interpreter whispered what was being said to an increasingly ill-at-ease Private Harrison. The more the mayor spoke, recounting his heroic exploits, the more that marine squirmed.

The mayor concluded his remarks by asking Private Harrison to stand beside him. Then with great ceremony, he presented him with a key to the city.

"That must be when that picture was taken," Noah said. "Can we see it again?"

"Yes, of course," M. Etienne said.

The three of them earnestly peered at the picture.

"I hadn't noticed, but they're shaking hands," Brea said.

"Yes, and if you look closely, you can see the mayor is holding out a key in his other hand. I found this picture when I read my father's entry, but I didn't stop to examine it."

"Did you notice that even though George is smiling, he looks uncomfortable. His smile seems fake," Noah said.

"I see what you mean. I hadn't noticed that before." They all stared again at the photo. "Monsieur Etienne, read us the rest. Why was he uneasy?"

Alexandre said, "Yes, let me continue."

When the mayor sat down, the marine asked if he could say a few words. He started by saying, "Merci beaucoup." Then, through his interpreter, he continued, "I appreciate all your kindness, but I am not a hero any more than the rest of you. I just happened to be in the right place at the right time. Any of you would have done the same as I did. It was just fortunate that, since I am a soldier, I am aware of German tactics and munitions. But, in truth, I am nothing special.

"I must tell you of someone who truly is special. Last month an Italian soldier, a messenger, was bringing information from his commander to the allied counterparts here in France. He saved my *life.*

"I was foolish. I had only been in France a short while, and I decided to go hunting for food—like that day I wandered into Viborgne. But somehow, I got turned around. So, stupidly, I was drawing closer to the front instead of farther away from it. As I was obliviously scrounging around, an Italian soldier yelled at me. I didn't understand what he was saying. He ran toward

me looking quite frantic. As he drew nearer, I heard a sniper bullet whiz past my head. Being new, I froze. That soldier tackled me, throwing me to the ground.

"He lay on top of me until the sniper fire let up and was replaced by cover fire from the other direction. I didn't look up until I felt his weight being lifted off me. Several American soldiers were crouching over us. After hauling away my Italian friend, they grabbed me and dragged me to safety.

"I was quite alarmed when they took off my shirt and I saw a large pool of blood on the back. 'No, no. Don't worry,' I was told. 'It is not your blood. It belongs to the man who was on top of you. He was shot in the gut.' I was stunned. 'Did he fall on you after he was shot?' they wanted to know.

"'No,' I was adamant, 'that man saved my life. He purposely jumped on me to save me from the sniper fire. He took the bullet that was meant for me.' I was grateful for what he did for me, but I was shocked and grieved that he was injured. My Italian rescuer was taken to a field hospital. I had to return to my unit. That's the last I heard of him. When I was helping your children, I was merely following his example."

Private George Harrison's story ended there. He had related such an astonishing series of events. Unlike what he said, I still saw him as an extraordinary hero. He had done for our town what was done for him. The fact that he tried to deflect duly-earned praise and ascribe it to another only made him grow in my esteem.

Alexandre closed the journal and held it in his lap. "Rereading this is like finding a long-lost friend. It has brought back the memory of hearing my father relate the same story to me when I was young. I can almost hear his voice in the words."

"That's incredible," said Brea. "Do you happen to know the name of the Italian?" She exchanged a meaningful glance with Noah.

"He does not say in the journal, and I do not recall him ever saying. I imagine George Harrison knew the Italian's name, but if he included it in his tale, my father did not recall it to my knowledge. It is only clear that he remembered the speech. It obviously made an impression on him even though he was merely eight at the time."

"Yes, I imagine so if he took the time to record it in his journal years later."

"That's crazy to think of," said Noah. "If the Italian had not saved George, then George couldn't have saved the children of Viborgne."

"No. He wouldn't have saved my father. Instead, my father could easily have died at the age of eight and his little sister certainly would have. I, among others, would not be here."

The impact of these thoughts hung in the air.

"When I was growing up, I remember the adults—the ones who were children during World War I—wishing they could see the American again to thank him. They were leading long, happy, productive lives which they feel were owed to his actions. And they were not wrong.

"That feeling of gratitude was ingrained in us as their children, although most of my generation have now forgotten or are no longer with us. I, however, will never forget that sense of gratitude. I am reminded of it every time I speak English since that is the reason I learned it.

"But I am surprised I forgot about the Italian. Now that my memory has been pricked, I recall that my father also wished he could see the Italian. He wanted to thank him, knowing that without him the other could not have been possible." Alexandre shook his head. "That happened 22 years before I was born. I am now 81 years old. The ripple from that one action is hard to fathom. I wish I could thank that Italian too. I doubt he ever knew the effect he had."

LEGACY

Before leaving, they exchanged contact information so they could stay in touch. "Thank you so much, Monsieur Etienne," Noah said. "We came to Europe so I could find out about George Harrison and what it meant that he was the Hero of Viborgne. I'm not sure I can thank you enough for what you've told us."

"You are most welcome, young man. Write to me. If you do, I promise to write back."

"I will."

Barely back in the car, Brea and Noah glanced at each other. "Mom, do you think he was talking about Beniamino?"

"The man was Italian, that's obvious. He was a messenger. I don't know how many messengers there would have been."

"But one going to France with a message? The Italians weren't in the battle of Château-Thierry or Belleau Wood, were they?"

"No. So, I'd think messengers from Italy to their allies here in France would be rare at that time."

"I know I came here for information about George Harrison, but if there's a connection to Benjamin Roberts, that would be so amazing." Noah was having a hard time containing his excitement.

"Both our mystery Italian and Beniamino were wounded in France."

"I know! It's got to be the same person."

"But there is the matter of the wound itself."

"What about the wound?"

"The story M. Etienne read to us said the Italian was shot in the gut. Beniamino's records, from the military and his wife, say he was shot twice, once in the leg and the other in the head. The nature of his injuries stood out to me because the official service record and my great-grandmother's journal were consistent. People don't always remember details accurately. That's why I took notice."

"Well, that's probably the answer then."

"What is?"

"You said, 'People don't always remember details accurately.' Monsieur Etienne's father wrote that years after it happened. It sounded like he was an adult, and he's remembering something from when he was eight years old. I'm sure he got things mixed up."

"Good point. Everything else matches up. We know Beniamino was treated here first, probably at a field hospital like the journal mentioned." They had been sitting in their rental car talking, so Brea finally turned on the ignition. "I don't know, Noah. It could be. I'm just not sure. Is there anything else you can think of? Any detail that might tie the two people together?"

They drove in silence for a few miles before Noah burst out, "Do you remember Hazel's journal that Grandma read us? She said Beniamino complained about the 'dumb Americans' he met in France. Mindlessly strolling around looking for food near the front lines of a war seems like a pretty dumb thing to be doing to me. Why else would he talk about the 'dumb Americans'? He wouldn't have interacted with them much."

"True. He would likely have passed along his message to the French commanders and then left. Dealing with any American forces wouldn't have been part of his job."

"Yeah, he was learning English, but that seemed like he was doing it for fun. He wouldn't have been trusted to speak with anyone important in English."

"You're right. I'm not certain, but it could have been him. I guess we'll never know for sure."

"Maybe not, but I think we can safely assume there was an Italian who saved George's life before he saved the children of Viborgne. There was a hero before the hero."

"Yes. Maybe you need to write something like that in your notebook of sayings."

Noah thought for a moment. "How about, 'Heroes are rarely the only hero'?"

"I like that. That seems worthy of your journal."

"Yeah. It's true though. Dad was a hero in the end, but he wouldn't have been one if you hadn't inspired him to want to be so."

"And he needed you to want to be a better dad."

"It's strange to think a little baby can make a difference. I like that idea. The way I've always heard the story is that Dad changed his mind and tried to back out because of the two of us."

"Yes. The only reason he was still part of the whole scam is because they threatened us. So, he stayed with it but sabotaged their efforts."

"I've heard that a lot before, but what it meant didn't register until I heard George's story. I guess that makes it easier to accept Dad as a hero."

"Why?"

"Because it wasn't all on him. He was flawed but you were pretty great, I assume, and we know I was amazing." He smiled broadly but quickly grew serious again. "Together, that makes enough to be a hero. He didn't have to shoulder all the responsibility of that himself. It's like George. He did something genuinely heroic, but the Italian set a great example for him. And who knows the impact that Italian's mother or a fellow soldier may have had on him. When we celebrate a hero, we're really celebrating all the people that influenced that person to be a hero. Any of those people, likely all of them, also have faults. But collectively, they still produced a hero."

"Heroes are rarely the only hero. I like your thoughts."

"I do too. Mimi was helping me accept Dad as a hero, but I still have to remind myself sometimes the things she said. But if I dismiss him as a hero, it would be like I was rejecting all our contributions too, and I don't want to do that. What he did was amazing. It took a lot of courage to change course like he did. And … he couldn't have done that alone."

When they arrived back at their hotel, Brea parked and glanced affectionately over at her son. "You're a great kid. I'm sure it hasn't been easy growing up without a dad physically present yet having the shadow of one impacting your life because of how he lived and died. You've handled that remarkably well. When you first told me you weren't sure your father was much of a hero, I wanted to correct you and set you straight. But I was reminded of my own struggles with that. It took time to heal and forgive him and then see him as the hero that he was. I worked through that so long ago, that it's easy to forget I took that journey and how necessary it was. I'm glad Martha, Mimi, was there to help you with that. And I'm sorry I wasn't."

"Don't be. Remember, heroes are rarely the only hero. You're my hero, Mom, but we both needed Mimi too. We can't, you can't, do it alone."

"Boy, kid, if I didn't know I was the parent, I'd swear you were. Now, come on. Let's go decide what to do with the rest of our day and what we want to do tomorrow."

"Mom, if it's okay with you, can you pick somewhere for dinner? And can we decide our future plans tomorrow? I'd like to spend the rest of the afternoon writing."

"Sure. The patio again?"

He grinned. "You know me too well."

• • •

Noah did not return to their room until it was time to leave for dinner. When he did, his demeanor was subdued but still cheerful. He carefully stowed his blue notebook among his things but offered no explanation as to what he'd written on its pages.

Brea fought the urge to ask. Instead, she said, "Are you ready to go?"

"Sure, as soon as I use the bathroom."

Sitting in the room by herself, waiting, she spied his notebook peeking out from among his things. She couldn't keep her eyes off it but was relieved she had no desire to break Noah's confidence and riffle through its pages.

"Okay, I'm ready."

She jumped at the sound of his voice. "I didn't know you were there. Let's go."

. . .

When they got back, it was late. They were both yawning. Brea wanted to make decisions and plans, but she could respect Noah's wishes and wait until morning.

After brushing her teeth, she climbed into bed. Noah was already in his bed, but he sat up when he saw her.

"Mom, I wrote a new poem. Would you like to hear it?"

She was suddenly wide awake. "Yes, I'd love to."

He beamed while retrieving his blue notebook. "I named it *Shadows* like the last one, but it's a completely different poem. Here it is."

Shadows
Legacies circle
*   Hero, heroes alone but no*
*   Casting shadows, making footprints*
Calling out
*   "Step into the light, son*
*   Step out of the shadows"*
How? How can I?
*   Step into my footsteps, my shadows*
*   I'll show you the way*
*   I've walked this path before*
*   I've blazed a trail*
*   Come, take my hand*
How? I can't see your hand
*   But you can*
*   In what I left behind*
*   In the way I loved — you love*
*   It's everywhere*
Legacies circle
*   Mimi, George, Alexander, Paul*
Echoes, Ripples

You can take my hand, our hands
You can
You can rise
You can rise above
Be better – than ever we were
"Step out of my shadow
Step into the light, my son!"

Brea sat on the bed stunned. "That's beautiful, Noah."

He beamed while silently replacing his notebook among his things. Then he climbed under his covers and fell asleep.

Brea lay awake, smiling, pondering his words.

THE ITALIAN

Over breakfast, Brea, eager to move forward, said, "So where now, Noah? Paris? The French Riviera? Somewhere else?"

He hesitated ever so briefly, but in that moment, she watched his face. By the time he said, "How about Paris? I've always heard about the Eiffel Tower and the Louvre," she knew his words left something out.

"Noah, I saw your face. What do you really want to do?"

He stared at her for a few moments before speaking. "If it's okay with you, I'd like to go back and see Monsieur Etienne again before we leave. He reminds me of Mimi and your mom and dad and Grandma and Grandpa Caste. I know he's not family, but he's lonely. He doesn't have family." He shrugged. "I don't know. What he told us means everything to me. I just–"

Brea put her hand on his shoulder and grinned. "You don't have to convince me. I think that's a great idea. I'm all in. Let me extend our reservation again and arrange to keep the car a little longer. That will only take a few minutes. Do you want to call him and tell him we're coming?"

"I was thinking we could just show up and surprise him. What do you think?"

"I think that would be lovely. I'm going to run down to the front desk. I've learned hand gestures work better than talking over the phone, unless Pierre answers. His English is probably better than mine."

Noah laughed. "While you're gone, I want to text Grandma and Grandpa Roberts and Grandma and Grandpa Caste. I haven't been great about staying in touch lately. I'm sure they're lonely too—even though they have each other."

"Any grandparent would be lonely when they haven't heard from their grandchild." Brea ruffled his hair. "But I suggest not sending more than one text each. It's the middle of the night there. You don't want to trigger an override of their do-not-disturb settings."

"Yeah, I forgot about that."

Brea was grateful to find Pierre at the front desk. He helped her extend her car reservation as well as their hotel stay. "Thank you so much."

"No problem. Let me know if you need anything else."

She walked into their room to find Noah ready to go. "No lazy morning, huh? You ready to go?"

"Yes, but not to Viborgne."

"What? I thought that's where we were headed."

"Yes, just not yet. I want to buy a present for Monsieur Etienne, and I have a great idea what to get."

"Okay, lead on then."

. . .

They visited several stores until Noah was satisfied they'd found the perfect version of what he was searching for. By then the sun was directly overhead.

"Should we grab something to eat and then head to Viborgne?"

"Yes, I'm starving."

They were waiting for their food when Noah's phone rang. "It's Grandma Caste!" He answered the phone, putting it on speaker so they could both hear. "Hi, Grandma."

"Hi, Mother Caste. We're both here, if you don't mind."

"Not at all, love. I just woke up, and the first thing I saw was Noah's text. What a wonderful way to greet the day! I have missed you two! It's so good to hear your voices. I know I don't see you all the time, but knowing you're half-way around the world breaks my grandma heart."

"I love you, Grandma."

"I love you too, Noah. Now tell me what you've been up to."

They were almost done with their meal by the time Noah caught Ava Caste up to date on their travels and all they'd discovered. "So, the thing we don't know now is whether the Italian was Beniamino Robustelli. But I guess only one mystery left isn't too bad."

"Not bad at all, especially considering how much you've learned. But I don't think it matters."

"Probably not. I just have to accept that we'll never know."

"No, I don't mean it that way, Noah. It doesn't matter if he's the hero, the one who saved George Harrison."

"Why do you say that?" Noah said, but Brea was wondering the same thing.

"The crucial point is there *was* a hero. Someone saved George so he could save the children and the town. And Benjamin was doing his part in the war effort which was every bit as valuable. His record is a little sparse on the details, from what you've told me, but it sounds like he was on an assigned mission when he was shot. You can be proud of him."

"Yeah. I guess you're right. He doesn't need to have a title like the Hero of Viborgne to be important. He was my great-great-grandfather. That's pretty cool."

"I like that," Brea said. "He made a difference for *me*—and for Noah."

"Why don't you go back to Viborgne," Ava Caste said. "Is it a small town?"

"Yes, it is."

"Then walk around the whole thing. Notice the people. Think about how they're there because George saved their grandparents and because someone saved George. One act of kindness had lasting ripple effects. And without your unknown hero, there would have been no Martha."

"Ripples," Brea said, "like your poem."

"What poem?" Grandma Caste asked.

"Oh, I'm sorry, Noah. I didn't mean to–"

"No, it's okay, Mom. Grandma, I've been doing some writing lately. I'll share some of my poems with you next time I see you."

"That's wonderful, Noah. I'd love to hear them."

"You're right about Martha too. We thought about that. But there's a whole town full of people that exist because of George and the Italian. It's funny that I thought of ripple effects, but I hadn't thought about ripples for other people."

"We often don't. It's easier to think about ourselves and the people we know by name. But whether that Italian was your relative or not, he mattered. George Harrison isn't a person that's known commonly in that town anymore, but he mattered. Anyone can make a difference."

"I like that. Anyone *can* make a difference. We were planning on going back to Viborgne to see Monsieur Etienne anyway, but I like your idea. It would be good to walk around. Mom?"

"I'm game."

"Thanks, Grandma."

"Yes, thank you, Mother Caste. We'll let you know how it goes."

. . .

A short time later, Brea and Noah emerged from their rental car into the center of Viborgne. As tempting as it was to pop into Le Marché de la Ville and visit Hugo, they'd decided on the way to start fresh where they knew no one, curious what they would see with new eyes. Yet they still parked close to the market so they could stop in and buy bread and cheese before they left.

Viborgne spread out from its city center. The town hall they visited earlier to comb through newspaper archives was on the east side of a beautiful town square. The grassed-in square featured a fountain at its center which was framed by a cobblestone walkway. Spaced along this walk were park benches. Brea and Noah had eaten lunch on one of those benches not many days before.

They strolled over to this city park and took a seat. A few children were playing in and around the fountain. It was small by European standards but impressive for Americans not accustomed to fountains in the middle of their small towns. The top tier spouted water into a large shell-like basin. Two cherubs crouched under the basin, shielding themselves, or more likely holding the basin on their shoulders. More water shot from beneath their feet into the larger pool below. The children circled it, laughing and trailing their hands in the water every few steps.

Noah nudged his mother and pointed out a small boy sitting on the ground next to the fountain. His blond hair was hanging across his forehead and into his eyes which sparkled with childlike inquisitiveness. He was holding a clover in his chubby hands. A fluffy white and black puppy was bounding around him, stopping to lick his face every few minutes. The boy's attention was on the clover, but he giggled whenever the puppy got near his face, and he would reach a hand out and pet the puppy's head.

Brea smiled wistfully. "He reminds me of you when you were little."

"Minus the puppy."

"Yes, you would bring that up again. Like I told you before, if you want a dog, we can work on that when we get home. Okay, so except for the puppy, that reminds me of you. You could become so enamored with the smallest things—an acorn, a shiny rock. That child is so young. He hasn't had a chance to make his mark on the world yet, but you know he's precious to his family." She looked at Noah and added, "Like you've always been precious to me."

As if on cue, a middle-aged woman approached the boy. "*Mamé, regarde ça!*" The child held the clover up for his grandmother to see. She admired it appropriately, handed it back, then reached for his hand. He took it, and with his free hand, he grabbed the puppy's leash. The boy skipped his way out of the park next to his grandma.

"Do you think she grew up in this town? The grandma?" Noah said.

"I don't know. She easily could have. It's probably a safe assumption."

"Then I'll go with that. Where to now?"

"Wherever you want. Lead the way, and I'll follow."

On the west of the square, opposite the town hall, was an old building with arched entryways. Whether it housed government offices, high-rent apartments, businesses, or something else, they couldn't tell. Large planters of bright red and purple blooms graced the sides of each entrance. As they strolled nearer, they noticed a man and woman approaching, carrying spades and flats of white and pink flowers.

As they watched, the two weeded and cleaned up the planters, removing any wilted flowers. Then they set about adding splashes of white and pink in amongst the red and purple. They worked smoothly and efficiently, like a doctor and surgical nurse in an operating room but with virtually no words passing between them as if they could read each other's minds.

The man noticed them standing nearby watching. He knit his brow. "*Qu'est-ce qui se passe?*"

Brea shrugged. "No French. Do you speak English?"

The woman lifted his head. "We speak a little."

"A little," the man added, holding two fingers close together to indicate just how much.

Noah pointed to their work. "Your flowers. They are beautiful."

Brea dug the English-French dictionary out of her bag to look up "flower" and "beautiful." The man shrugged, but the woman walked over to her and touched her hand, "It is okay. I understand." She was smiling. "*Merci.*"

"Do you live in Viborgne?"

"Yes," she said.

"Have you always lived here?"

"Always? No." Brea's and Noah's faces fell until she added, "But my grandmother lives here always."

"Was she born here? In Viborgne?"

"Yes. She was born 1945. My family has lived here long time. Many generations."

"Many generations?" Brea repeated. "That's wonderful!" She squealed with delight.

. . .

"That is so cool, Mom. She's alive because of George even though she knows nothing about him."

They had walked away from the pair after thanking them for their time. The couple had nodded but with puzzled expressions, clearly mystified by Brea's reaction.

"They must think I'm some stupid, crazy American, but I don't care," Brea said.

"I reserve the right to be embarrassed by my mother, but at the moment, I'm with you. I don't care what they thought."

They wandered around the square to the church at its northern end. "Should we go in, Noah?"

"Sure. This is the first image I saw when googling Viborgne—the church. It must be a symbol of the town."

"That's probably true of most old towns. But for us this particular church, I remember, was the first thing to tie Viborgne to World War I because of its damaged steeple."

They both tipped their heads up to gaze at the steeple on the top.

"It is an impressive steeple," Noah said.

They walked through the gate that surrounded the church yard. An old cemetery occupied the area to the left of the church, extending for some distance behind it. "Those headstones look really old," said Noah.

"Some of them *are*," a deep voice said.

Brea and Noah turned to find the source of the words—a priest standing at the top of the church steps. He was in the open doorway and smiling at them, his old, wizened face appearing friendly.

"You speak English?" Noah said.

"Yes. I lived much of my life in England. I heard your question and your American accents—not something I hear very often. I hope you can understand my British one. I am Père Martin, Father Martin."

"Your accent is lovely, actually," Brea said. "I'm Brea Cass, and this is my son, Noah."

"Welcome, welcome. It is so nice to meet you." He closed the church door behind him and descended the steps. "So, can I help you with anything?"

"Yes," said Noah. "You said there are old headstones. Are there any back as far as World War I?"

Father Martin threw back his head and laughed. "You Americans think 100 years old is ancient. The graves from World War I are in the modern section. We have graves back several hundred years. But if you'd like to see those from World War I, I can help you."

"Oh. Yeah, that would be great."

"Are you trying to find an ancestor of yours who served in The Great War?" he said as he led them to a corner of the graveyard.

"Not really, no."

"That's good because most of those headstones are in the cemeteries around Château-Thierry. Most of our soldiers' graves are local boys. So, what or who are you looking for then?"

"It's complicated."

The priest stopped by a section of headstones with several small French flags planted in the ground. "Here it is. Do you want to wander around ... or would you like to explain what, 'It's complicated,' means?"

"Sorry, we're not really looking for anyone in particular buried here," Brea said.

"We came to Viborgne because a friend's father served around here. He didn't die in the war, thank goodness. But he was known as the Hero of Viborgne. That's what brought us here," Noah added.

"Really? I've never heard of that before."

"Not surprising," Brea said. "We discovered it's not well known. He was here during World War I. It's left us curious about that war. You don't hear much about it. It's overshadowed by World War II, although they were both horrific."

"Yes, they were. Both were hard on this town. The World War II graves are over there," he said, pointing to the left. "This is a small town. People are born here, live here, die here. These graves are visited often by family members, sometimes descendants, most often by relatives because the young soldiers didn't live long enough to have offspring of their own."

"That's sad," said Noah. "While we've been here, we learned about an Italian soldier that saved our friend's father, who saved children in this town. We've been thinking about how many people are alive because of that. It's sad that others weren't so lucky."

"Yes," Father Martin said. "Did you say an Italian soldier? Do you happen to know his name?"

"Yes and no. I mean, yes, it was an Italian soldier, but we don't know his name."

"There's an Italian buried here in the World War I section—one of the few graves that doesn't belong to a local. Any American or Belgian would be buried in the military cemeteries close by. Italians were rare around these parts at that time. They served in France but not often around here. It's an oddity, but I admit I've never been curious enough about that Italian to examine his records."

"Can you show us his headstone?"

"Of course. He's right over here." He walked them to a lonely corner where an old, neglected grave stood. The headstone was slightly askew. "It never has flags or flowers. That's how I first noticed it—because it appeared to be *un*noticed by everyone else."

"It reminds me of the leaning tower of Pisa." Noah said, but then his face grew somber. He bent over and traced the man's name just as he'd done with Martha Harrison Fereday before leaving home. "His name was Marcello Ricci." He glanced up at his mom, his eyes wide. "Do you think he's the one?"

Brea knelt beside him. "He died in 1918. Father Martin, what is this month? *Juillet?*"

"*Juillet* means July. The other month, *Août*, is August."

"Then he died July 3, 1918. That means he was here at the right time. His birthdate was August 12, 1895. That would make him 22 years old, not quite 23."

"Who do you think he was?" Father Martin asked.

"If we're right, his grave should be the most decorated of any of them. We came here searching for information about George Harrison. He's the one we mentioned who was called the Hero of Viborgne. He saved the town's children from mustard gas the Germans left behind when they retreated. But before he did that, an Italian saved him."

Brea took over his tale. "They would both have been here around the time of the Battle of Château-Thierry. This death date matches that time frame. The Italian tackled George when he was in the line of fire, taking the bullet meant for George. From what we heard, he was shot in the stomach, but we weren't sure we believed that account. Another Italian was here at the same time under similar circumstances. He was also shot, but in the leg and the head. We figured the two Italians could be the same person given faulty memories with the passage of time. But if they actually were two separate people ... well, a stomach wound could have easily been fatal. He might never have made it home."

"Let me check our records to see if we have any information about this young man. I will be back shortly. Our records are very orderly. If there is something to learn, I'll be able to find it quickly."

"Thank you," Brea said.

They sat down together in front of Marcello's headstone. Noah leaned his head on his mother's shoulder. "I don't know if it's him, but it feels like it is. We never knew him, but he was real. He did something so brave, and he probably died without ever knowing how amazing he was. His family probably never even knew how he died or what he did."

They sat in solemn silence. Noah reached out again to trace the name: Marcello Ricci. Hearing the swish of the priest's footsteps as he approached, they lifted their heads expectantly to him.

"Sometimes our records list date of death, date of burial—that type of information. But more detailed records do exist on occasion." He smiled at them. "This was one of those occasions. Would you like to come with me into the church? The record is inside in a large volume. It is, of course, in French. But I can translate it for you."

Somberly, Brea and Noah followed Father Martin inside. The church was not ornate like some they had seen, but it was still composed of repeating Gothic arches that gave it an open, peaceful feel, being beautiful in both its grandeur and simplicity. Their footsteps echoed as they walked up the aisle toward an office near the front and off to one side.

"Please, have a seat," Father Martin beckoned once they were inside the office. He had a large, old volume opened on the desk. "Everything is entered chronologically. We have baptism, marriage, and burial records back hundreds of years." He waved his arm to indicate the volumes and volumes behind him and on neighboring shelves. Many of them appeared to be ancient.

"When there is more information—something unusual, perhaps—it is entered in a separate book, but a notation is made in the ledger so we know to look it up. It is a system that was started by the first priests of this parish, and it is one we still use today."

"The notation about Marcello Ricci led me here. It was recorded by Father Durand." He turned the book around so they could see the long entry. It was written in a beautiful, legible hand. While it was written in French, the name Marcello Ricci was clearly visible at the top.

The priest turned the book back to himself, cleared his throat, and began to translate.

On the afternoon of July 3rd, 1918, a young Italian in uniform stumbled into the back of the church. He was badly wounded and collapsed before he could make it to where I was near the altar. I summoned an altar boy to help, and we managed to get him into a nearby pew. I immediately wanted to send for a doctor, but the Italian soldier stopped me. He spoke French and told me he had just come from a field hospital. He needed to find a church and confess before he died as he did not want his soul to go to Hell. I could see that the man's torso was expertly bandaged, giving credence to his story of the field hospital. However, blood had seeped through and was spreading. I again pleaded with the young man to let me send the altar boy for help. He finally relented but begged me to stay with him.

When the altar boy left, the Italian, whose name I learned was Marcello Ricci, insisted I give him last rites. Then he told me his story. He was wounded in the belly when he took a bullet for an American soldier. "I only hope he lives a long life," he said. "Maybe then, in some way, it will make up for my mistakes." He brushed aside my questions about his heroics, saying, "I'll get to that, but it is not the important part of my story." He had a hard time talking because his injury was sapping him of strength.

"I was sent on a mission with an important message to be delivered to the French military leaders near here," he said. "My companion and I made the journey quickly, but the fighting here made it difficult to return safely. So, rather than leave right away, the French commanders asked that we stay. That way we would be able to report back to our general with information about the results of the battle. The fighting was intense, but they hoped to win soon with the help of the newly arrived Americans.

"My companion and I took advantage of our unexpected vacation to explore France farther back behind the battle lines. Our first day, I met Lisette. She was beautiful and kind. My heart was on fire whenever she was near. I snuck out every day to see her. My friend was at first amused, but he soon became weary of my love-sick talk and ways. He was growing anxious to return to General Colombo and report. Despite the French leaders' objections, he was determined to find a way around the battle and return with updated maps and information. As soon as that talk began, I made plans with Lisette. I was going to desert and run away with her. My companion got wind of my intentions and begged me not to. He tried to talk sense into me, but I refused to listen.

"So, in the middle of the night, I took off, but before morning, he had tracked me down at Lisette's. He forcibly hauled me back to our tent near the front and tried once again to talk to me. I broke free and ran. When he chased me, I turned and shot him twice. I don't know if I killed him. I just

ran. That's when I came across that stupid American. If I hadn't been so consumed with guilt over what I had just done, I might have left him blindly stumbling into harm's way. But I couldn't. I had to rescue the fool. And for my trouble, I got shot. I hope it makes up for probably killing my friend Beniamino Robustelli. Curse him! Curse him! I should have been off with my girl instead of getting shot for a Yank. But even still, I am sorry. I am sorry." He barely got out those last words before dying on the pew right in front of me. When the altar boy returned with a medic, all he could do was shut his eyes.

When I had urged Marcello to let me send for a doctor, he calmly said he knew he was dying and asked to be laid to rest here. He was too ashamed to be sent home. I did not know if he had actually committed murder. It was wartime after all. So, we buried him in the church yard.

Father Martin sighed. "It is signed, Father Durand." He reverently closed the volume and glanced up at his two guests. Both were crying.

"Heroes are rarely the only hero," Noah whispered to his mother, who nodded.

"Father Martin," Brea said, "Marcello Ricci was not a murderer. Beniamino Robustelli did not die."

"How do you know?"

"He was my great-grandfather."

NO REGRETS

"I might need to make a notation in that book after what you just told me," Father Martin said. "I imagine Father Durand's soul will rest easier knowing he did not bury a murderer in sacred ground. Not to mention Marcello's soul." He smiled kindly. "But I imagine they have met each other on the other side and worked things out for themselves."

"Thank you for sharing it with us. It gave us answers we thought we would never have," Noah said.

"You are most welcome. Would you like to photograph this record? It is obviously in French, but–"

"Yes! That would be a priceless treasure," Brea said.

Father Martin beamed. "I am pleased to have helped."

Once Brea had finished taking pictures, Father Martin said, "Would you like to look around the church? I'd be happy to be your tour guide. It was completed in the year 1225, during the early Gothic period."

"I would love to," said Brea.

"Go ahead," said Noah. "I think I'd like to go back to Marcello Ricci's grave."

"I can–"

"Mom, it's okay. Take a tour of the church. I'll be at his graveside when you're done. I'd like to be alone until then."

She nodded and watched him go. Turning back to the priest, she said, "Thank you so much, Father Martin. You've given us more than knowledge. I believe it's healing balm as well."

. . .

Nearly an hour later, Brea walked through the grass to find Noah sitting cross-legged in front of Marcello Ricci's headstone. It was late afternoon. They would need to get going soon to allow time for a proper visit with Alexandre Etienne.

She approached somewhat noisily so as not to startle Noah. But he did not turn at the sound of her coming. So, she took a place next to him on the grass and waited for him to speak.

"I miss her." His voice was quavering. He lifted his tear-stained face to meet her gaze. "I miss Mimi. I miss her so much." He buried his head in his hands.

She put an arm around him and held him close. When his breathing slowed, Noah said, "Marcello died with regrets. And he didn't know what happened to Beniamino or what George was destined to do. He had a whole plateful of unfinished business. Even Lisette was a loose end. It makes me sad to think about.

"But seeing his headstone, tracing the letters of his name—that reminds me of Mimi. She lived a good life. I doubt she had any regrets. But I wasn't ready for her to go! I know she was dying and she was old, but I wasn't ready!" He buried his head in his hands again.

Brea rubbed his back, leaning her head against his. "You haven't mourned her until now, have you?"

He shook his head. "I was too busy being *responsible*, trying to be the perfect kid for you." His voice dripped with disdain. "I know we've talked about not needing to be perfect. I'm working on that. But I didn't realize until now that because of that I never cried over Mimi when she died. At first, I was just numb. And then … well, then I thought I needed to be even stronger than before because you didn't have Mimi, your Martha, anymore. I guess I screwed it all up, didn't I?"

"Noah, you didn't screw up anything. This is hard. Life is hard. And it's okay to be sad. It's okay to mourn and to miss her."

Noah wiped his eyes. "Honestly, Mom, it feels good to cry. In a strange way, it makes me happy. Does that make any sense? It's like even though I was trying to be strong for you, I also thought I was a horrible person for not crying about Mimi. I thought I must be a real jerk. But, I'm not, am I?"

"You are not! You're an amazing kid. Noah, grieving is complicated. Everyone does it in their own way and in their own time. The fact that you're doing it is a positive thing. Cry, sob, talk about it, write about it. But, above all, let it come. Don't hide it or bury it."

"Thanks, Mom."

"Do you just want to go back to the hotel? Alexandre isn't expecting us, so we can come back another day."

"No!" The strength of his response startled Brea. "No, Mom. He's lonely. I want to go see him today. It feels like I'll be doing it for Mimi."

"Okay. If you're up for it, let's do it."

"Mom, I'm sure Mimi didn't have any regrets, but do you think she had unfinished business? I sometimes wonder if she had more to tell me about Dad before she died because we were talking about him right up until the end."

"I don't know about that, Noah. I couldn't say. Maybe giving us those envelopes was a way for her to make sure any possible unfinished business didn't stay that way."

"You think so?"

"I do. You know Martha. She always thought of everything."

"She did." He wiped his eyes again. "Do you think she knew … about the article? Do you think it was stuck to the bottom of the box on purpose? That it would lead to all this?"

Brea shook her head. "I have no idea. She would often say, 'I just had a feeling …' But I don't know. I think that's one question that will never be answered."

Noah could only nod in agreement.

. . .

They stood with nervous excitement on Alexandre Etienne's front step. Brea was holding bread and cheese they'd purchased with Hugo's help, and Noah was holding their gift, carefully wrapped in tissue paper.

"*J'arrive, j'arrive*," Alexandre's voice called from deep inside the house. When he swung open the door, his mouth dropped. "*Ooh là là!* My goodness! It is my American friends. I did not think I would see you again. I am so pleased! Come in, come in."

"We brought cheese and bread. It may not be much for supper, but we didn't want to wait longer into the evening before we came," Brea said, extending their purchases to him.

"But, ah! I have made a pot of soup. I always make a big pot so I can eat it over several days. So, there is plenty for all of us."

"But we don't want to take your soup from you."

He flashed a sly grin and winked. "I said I eat it over several days. I didn't say I liked eating it over several days." He laughed. "Don't worry. I am a good cook."

They followed the chuckling Alexandre to the kitchen adjacent to the cozy den they visited before. A small, round table sat in the corner with two chairs. He excused himself, returning shortly with a third chair.

Before long, they were all hungrily eating soup, bread, and cheese. "This is delicious, Monsieur Etienne," Brea said.

"Please, call me Alexandre. You've seen the flower garden out front. But I also have a vegetable garden out back. The beef in the soup is from the butcher, but most of the vegetables I grew myself. Some of the herbs are mine as well." He pointed to a variety of herbs growing in his kitchen window.

"Did your wife start you growing those too?" Noah asked.

"Ah, my wife. Yes. You remembered about her flowers. She also tended to the herbs, but the vegetables were ours together. I grew up tending a garden with my father. Now I get a neighbor boy to help me with it since my joints don't work like they used to. I plant more than I need, and he takes home the excess to his *maman* and family."

They chatted like old friends as they enjoyed the evening meal together. When they finished, Alexandre produced a box of chocolates which they passed around until it was empty.

"We have something we would like to give you," Noah said, retrieving the tissue-wrapped gift from his lap. "Here."

Alexandre glanced from Noah to Brea, but they gave away nothing, simply nodding toward the package. He gently unwrapped it to reveal a scarf. His face burst into a broad grin.

"May I tie it on your arm and take a picture?" said Brea.

He laughed. "Of course, but only if we take a picture of all three of us."

They took many photos—of each other, of the scarf tied on each person's arm, and group shots kindly taken by a helpful neighbor. They scrolled through the finished products in Alexandre's den, pleased with the results.

"There is something more, Alexandre," Brea said. "We have more of the story to tell you."

Over the course of the next half hour, as they sipped on tea, Brea and Noah took turns telling him about Beniamino Robustelli and their visit to the church cemetery. When they told him of Marcello Ricci, he repeated the name to himself.

"It appears I should be thanking your Beniamino. I should be giving you this scarf." Then before they could refuse, he added, "But I know that will not do. I must write down those two names. And I will visit Marcello's lonely grave. It will not be without flowers ever again. Through me, you have fulfilled my father's wish—to be able to thank that young soldier. You have made an old man very happy."

Alexandre rose from his chair and retrieved his father's journal, the volume he read from on their last visit. "I would like you to have this journal. Some of it will not be of interest, but it has the entry about the Italian Marcello Ricci."

"We couldn't take that."

"Who else would care? I do not have children. I have nieces and nephews, but they are not interested in this history. It is important to you. It ties your people together—your George with Marcello. And the church record ties Marcello to your Beniamino. Please, take it." He thrust it to them.

Brea took it from his outstretched hand but said, "How about I take pictures of it. Then we will have the story, but you will have the journal with all that your father had to say during that time."

Alexandre threw up his arms. "I cannot argue with a beautiful woman. But I will insist on one thing. Excuse me a moment."

They heard him rummaging around in a room down the hall. When he returned, he handed a delicate, white item to each of them. "These are French lace doilies. They have been in my family for generations. You must not refuse this gift. Brea, use it in your home to remember me. And Noah, yours is for your future wife. Tell her it is hers because of your Great-Great-Grandfather Beniamino Robustelli and your friend's father George Harrison, and your friend Alexandre Etienne." He reached over and ruffled Noah's hair like Brea so often did.

OF SUPERHEROES

The warm glow of their evening with Alexandre lingered as Brea and Noah drove back to their hotel. Despite the sadness of the day, there was much to celebrate. They chatted happily about what they had learned, experienced, felt, enjoyed.

As they drew closer to the hotel, Brea was talking more and Noah was talking less, but it escaped her notice. When she turned off the ignition, Brea was surprised to see Noah staring at her. "What? What's up?"

"I have one more confession to make," he lowered his eyes.

"Noah? What is it? I thought you'd told me everything." She was trying to remain calm but not succeeding in keeping the trepidation out of her voice.

Instead of answering, Noah said, "Could we go on a walk?"

The night was warm, but a wayward breeze tugged at their clothes and tousled their hair as they meandered along the streets near their hotel. Still, Noah did not elaborate as they walked on in silence.

Brea, in an effort not to rush her son, directed her attention to the minute details of each building they passed. Every cornice, window, archway had been created with meticulous care and great patience. The accompanying awe helped slow her rapidly-beating heart, and her hands unclenched. Noah had started a conversation, and she knew he would see it through—if she was careful not to shut him down.

As they completed a loop that brought them back near the entrance of their hotel, Brea pointed out a bench. Noah nodded and they settled onto it.

"What is it, Noah? Whatever it is, I'll listen."

He squirmed in his seat. "I didn't tell you everything. I just told you there was nothing else you needed to worry about."

"Okay. I guess you did say it that way, didn't you?" But worry was exactly what Brea was doing.

"We even agreed you didn't need to know all my secrets."

"That's true. But if there's something you want to tell me …"

Noah took a deep breath. "I promise it's nothing bad. I've been saving my allowance and taking pottery classes. I saw them advertised at the library."

Brea raised her eyebrows. "That was not what I was expecting. That's your big secret? I'm not sure I understand. Classes don't strike me as something to be concerned about, but why didn't you tell me? That part does worry me a little." Then before he could object, she held up her hand to stop him. "I'm working on it, okay? But hiding where you're going is a parental red flag. Surely, you can understand that."

"Yeah, I get it. That's why I wanted to come clean now. I didn't tell you when I signed up because you still thought I was hanging out with friends. And I couldn't tell you I'd lost my friends without telling you how that happened." Brea nodded, so he continued. "I've been working on ceramics projects—a bowl, a pot, the usual. I made excuses about why I needed to leave my work there instead of taking it home. I'm not great at it, but they're not bad."

"I'd love to see what you've made, but I noticed you changed topics. Noah, I understand why you hid it initially. But why didn't you tell me when you fessed up about the party and hanging out at the library?" She was making an effort to keep the edge out of her voice so he wouldn't shut down. "I don't understand why this was such a big deal."

He glanced down at his hands. "I've been wondering that myself, why I was reluctant to tell you about the pottery. I think I finally figured it out." He lifted his head to meet her gaze. "It's because it's completely unrelated to computers."

"Computers?"

"Yeah, you know, yours and Dad's thing—computers." He shrugged like the connection was obvious.

"Noah, I am an intelligent woman, but I'm still lost. What are you talking about? Taking a pottery class is nothing compared to that party. So, I don't understand why this was the bigger secret."

He sighed. "The point is, it's nothing like what Dad would do or what he did." Grimacing, he added, "But hiding it kind of was. I'm sorry about that."

Brea didn't respond. But she maintained eye contact as an invitation for him to continue.

"The truth is I've hated and resented Dad for a long time. I told you Mimi was helping me see him in a different light. But I didn't tell you how angry I was to start with. Dad got himself killed because he did something bad. The whole hero thing … it bothered me. I don't have a father and you don't have a husband because of his choices."

"But–"

"No, don't defend him. I told you that's why I talked to Mimi about him, because she was Switzerland. She was neutral. I was finally comfortable with how I felt about Dad when Mimi died, but it was a fragile peace. I was teetering. My feelings could easily go either way. Taking pottery classes was a way to distance myself from Dad, and kind of you too. I'm sorry about that, but I knew you wouldn't understand my anger. I thought I'd set it aside by then, but I was so afraid it would come back with Mimi gone.

"When I saw the article about George, I wanted to learn everything I could about him. I wanted to know what a real hero looked like. I've been struggling with that ever since. I know I told you I didn't really know why that article caught my attention or that it was because of Mimi, but the truth is it was about Dad. I just didn't want to tell you that."

Brea said nothing but put her hand on Noah's. They sat in silence for several minutes.

Timidly, Noah said, "Mom, I told Matteo and Carlo about Dad, but I probably wasn't fair in what I told them. I figured they would understand, and I think I wanted them to tell me they resented their dad too."

When he didn't continue, Brea gently prodded, "What did they say? Do they resent him?" She wasn't sure what the response would be or even what she wanted it to be.

"They said the answer wasn't that simple." He pulled out his phone. "This is what Carlo wrote:"

We loved our padre. But the responsibility his death placed on our shoulders was heavy. We felt the need to take his place, and we didn't know how to do it. What child would? It's hard enough to be an adult when you actually are one.

"He said some more stuff, but that was the most important to me. Instead of distancing myself from Dad, I'm beginning to feel more like we're in this together."

Brea nodded and opened her mouth to speak, but Noah wasn't finished.

"Matteo responded to me too, but instead of telling me stuff, he asked me questions about Dad and what happened when he died. No one has asked me questions like that before. Everyone else around me knows more about what happened with Dad than I do. So, I was on the other side of it for once. Explaining it to him helped me see it better myself."

He paused, looking off into the distance. "Hero is such a strange word. In some ways, I see Matteo and Carlo as heroes with how they take care of their mom, even if that's not our usual definition of the word. Dad was and wasn't a hero. I thought for a moment Beniamino was a hero, then he wasn't, then he was. I mean, he turned out to be a hero just not the one I expected. If he hadn't stood up to his friend, Marcello wouldn't have been in the right place at the right time. I know I said heroes aren't the only heroes, but it's more than that. Heroes don't have to be amazingly heroic or even perfect to be heroes, do they? Marcello was trying to desert, but he ended up becoming a reluctant hero.

"I guess what I'm saying is Dad became a hero even if he was a flawed person. And he did it because he was trying not to be that flawed person anymore. I can see now how someone can be decent and honorable even if they have issues, but they're trying."

"That's a good way to view it."

"I wish I could say I came up with that myself, but I didn't. When Matteo finished asking questions about Dad, he told me something I've thought a lot about. Here, read this." Noah handed his phone to his mom.

"This email?" When Noah nodded, Brea started reading aloud:

Noah,

I've had to look up a few English words to write this, so I hope it makes sense. The title hero sounds like superhero, and we know those don't really exist. Heroes are people we idealize, which means they are the ideal, the ultimate at something. But that's not possible, just like superheroes aren't possible. No one could be the very best, the perfect example of anything unless they are a fictional character. Real people make mistakes. This is true. So, maybe hero should mean something else.

When you wrote us about your dad, it didn't sound right—not the facts but the way you said them. You were trying too hard to be angry. Carlo will tell you I played angry for a while, but it didn't work. That's why I asked you about your dad. Carlo did the same with me. When you answered my questions, you told me the truth about how you feel. I could tell you were proud of how your dad tried to fix things. You started to defend him and his actions to me. You forgot to be angry.

Stop expecting your dad, even your dad the hero, to be perfect. Then maybe you'll stop expecting yourself to be perfect too.
Ciao,
Matteo

"Wow," Brea said. "That makes me wish I'd said that."

"Yeah. It makes a lot of sense. I've read it several times. It's helping. Mom, I'm sorry I didn't tell you about the pottery lessons. They were my way of rebelling against Dad, and he's not even here to rebel against. It's hard to fight a ghost. And I guess it's hard for you to help me when I'm fighting that ghost."

Brea nodded. "I'm guessing you're coming to realize there's no actual ghost you need to fight. Am I right?"

"Yeah, I think so. Dad … well, he was a real person. He isn't the idealized hero to me anymore, but he was very heroic. I can live with."

"Yes, I can too. Thanks for telling me. I came to the same conclusion about your father and his hero status, but I never put it into words the way you and Matteo just did. Thank you."

"And Mom? I'm sorry I didn't tell you the real reason I had to come to Viborgne."

Brea squeezed his hand. "I understand."

ENVELOPE #6 AGAIN

The night wrapped around them as they sat on their bench in much the way a blanket does after a long, tiring day. They tipped their heads together, drinking in the peaceful atmosphere.

"Noah, this is ironic, you know."

"What is?"

"Before this trip I was so worried about what you were hiding from me. Honestly, Riley's party was the sort of thing most parents dread. So, when you told me about that, I figured the only thing left to worry about was finding a way to reconnect with you." She paused, collecting her thoughts. "Don't get me wrong, those are things I want you to tell me about, and we've figured out 'the whole apple thing,' and talking on Sundays. All of that's important, but it wasn't what you were really hiding from me. I didn't know you were so angry about your dad. Maybe if I'd been more open about talking with you about him, it would have been different. But maybe not. I'm glad you finally let me know. It sounds trite to say something like, 'You know you can always talk to me.' That's harder to do than it sounds, but we can try, can't we?"

"Yeah, we can."

"I'm sorry your dad didn't survive—to see you grow up, to be here for you. Things would have been so different if he had. That's a hole we've all been trying to fill. You've been trying to create a memory of a man you didn't know. I've been trying to be both Mom and Dad, and Mimi was trying to fill in the gaps. It's time to stop trying to do the impossible. I'm sorry it wasn't different, but being sorry doesn't change anything."

"Not really. But I don't think Mimi was filling in the gaps. I think she was trying to convince me there wasn't a hole in the first place." He looked plaintively at his mother. "Why did she have to die?"

"Oh, Noah, I miss her too."

"It's like when she died, Dad died for me too. She started what Matteo helped me finish. She was helping make him real—not a saint and not some villain, just a human being. We talked about the whole hero thing, but she also talked about what he was like every day. She told me her first impressions of him and how concerned he was about you when you were pregnant with me. I miss Mimi, but I also miss Dad. Or I miss the thought of him, the decent person he was most days and the incredible person he was becoming. Can you cry over the death of someone you don't really know?"

"I don't see why not." Brea pulled him close. "If you can wait six months to grieve Mimi, I don't see any reason you can't wait twelve years to grieve your father. You were too young then to understand. But that's not the case anymore."

"Thanks, Mom." With his head against her shoulder, he let the silent tears come—for Mimi and for his dad.

Brea tipped her head onto Noah's. Softly she said, "I still miss him. I miss them both."

"You know, I was worried I'd start resenting Dad all over again after Mimi died. But I'm not angry anymore. It didn't come back, I guess thanks to George and Matteo—and you. Dad's life mattered, even if it ended too soon. It's just hard not to wish there was more to his story."

Brea suddenly sat upright. "I can't believe I forgot. Noah, we both know your dad can't add to his story. That's sad and tragic. The real problem, however, is you've felt disconnected from what story there was. But, Noah, I wrote it down! When you were a toddler, I wrote his story—the positives and the negatives. It's not unbiased, but it includes everything to the best of my knowledge. I wrote it to help me make sense of the two sides of him. It's as much about my journey to understand him as it is about him."

Noah was drying his tears, trying to understand what his mother was telling him. "Do you still have it?"

"Yes! It's on my computer. It's one of those old files that I carry over every time I buy a new computer. I wrote it when the details and events were fresh in my mind. I didn't hide his betrayal and the pain it caused, but I included the love I felt and how I was able to forgive him and why."

"Could I read it?"

"Of course." Her eyes flew open wide. "Noah! Oh, my goodness! Martha told me to share with you what I've written and why I wrote it. That was the last envelope I opened. It was great to talk to you about code I've written, but this is what I really needed to share with you. I can't believe I didn't think of that before."

"I would like to read it. That would mean a lot to me." As he considered the possibilities, he added, "That's something I can read on my own, with my own thoughts."

"And if you find parts you want to reread or digest over time, you can."

"Without feeling like I'm bugging you. This is amazing."

"It is, isn't it? Martha thought of everything, didn't she?"

Noah nodded. "So, what about the other part of Martha's instructions? Why did you write it?"

"Honestly, I felt compelled to write it. Life was moving on, and with it the memories were fading. I was afraid if I didn't write them down, they would be lost. It's easy to forget how important it is to write our stories. Nicolas, Alexandre's dad, writing his journal is a great reminder of that."

"And Beniamino and especially Hazel."

"Right. You should write down George's story, all the parts of it—for you and for Martha. I'm sure it would be valuable to her children, and it would be a nice way to honor her memory."

"I agree, but that doesn't sound like much of an answer. It's too general. Is there anything else?"

"Isn't that sufficient?"

"I don't know. Dad's story is complicated. It just seems like the answer to why you wrote it would be complicated too." He eyed her, waiting for a response.

Brea huffed in frustration. Gradually tears began to pour down her face. "I wrote it because I needed to remember that things are messy. They're complicated, like you said. Life isn't always pretty; sometimes it's ugly and dirty. But even when it is, I can survive. I can thrive. I can forgive. I can love. I wanted to include *all* the details, both sides of the equation. I wrote about everything up to your first birthday. It's a love story, a 'true' love story—not like 'true love,' but like the truth about love, or at least my experience with it. I love your father deeply, even to this day. But saying I love him doesn't begin to cover the range of emotions that go with that. I didn't want to forget the breadth and depth of that, the power of such love." She wiped at her eyes. "I haven't read it for years. I think it's time I did again."

Taking a deep breath, she added, "Okay, can we agree to be all cried out for one day?"

Noah chuckled. "I think so. Let's go inside, okay?"

Opening the door to their room, Noah hesitated. "Do you have Dad's story on your laptop? The one you brought with you?"

"I do. I told you, I always transfer that story."

"Is it really the complete, unvarnished truth?"

"Yes, it is."

"And you haven't changed it since then?"

"Nope. All I ever did was fix typos. The story is just as I wrote it then. It helped me make sense of my life. It wouldn't have been right to modify that." She watched his face. "Would you like me to pull it up now?"

Noah nodded. Only moments later, he was staring transfixed at the file on the screen.

Brea moved away so he could read it by himself. "When we get home, I'll put it on your computer or print it out, if you want. I'll warn you, it's long. I didn't want to leave anything out."

"Good." He started to read but paused. "Mom?"

"Yes?"

"Thanks. I needed this."

"You're welcome."

"One last thing, Mom."

"I'm listening."

"Now that I have this to read, we're good. You don't need to be Mom and Dad. You don't need to carry the weight of what Dad did and didn't do. Your words will do that. So, live your life, please."

She stared into his eyes for a long time. Slowly, a tear trickled down her cheek. "I thought we agreed to be done with tears for today," she quietly said.

"I'm not going to apologize for that one. You need to know you're not just Mom, you're Brea. Go be Brea."

She nodded, too choked up for words.

ENVELOPE #7

The train from Chateau-Thierry to Paris took about an hour. Brea leaned her head back and slept the time away, emotionally spent.

Noah had stayed up late the night before reading about his father, but he was too energized to nap on the train. He sat perched on the edge of his seat, reading from his mother's laptop. Before he was ready, they arrived in Paris, and he had to pack it away.

Brea had booked them into a posh hotel in the center of Paris. They planned to stay for several days, but she pushed no agenda on Noah when they first arrived. She instead chose to quietly settle in, letting him read and digest the events from a dozen years before.

"Noah, what would you like for dinner? I can go get us something."

"Whatever you want, Mom, is fine with me," he said before returning to his reading.

She wandered out onto their balcony with its wrought-iron railing, observing the busy Paris street below. She checked out the indoor pool which she found to be far more elegant than the one at the Summerhill Budget Hotel near home. Eventually, she ventured onto the boulevard in front of the hotel, following it to several restaurants recommended by the hotel staff.

When she returned with samplings from two of those restaurants, she was surprised to find her laptop closed and her son nowhere in sight. "Noah?" She peered into the bathroom and around the room one more time. "Noah?"

"I'm here, Mom." His voice came from the balcony.

He had moved two chairs outside and was sitting in one of them. "The weather's nice. I thought you might like eating outside. What do you think?"

"Great idea. I have enough food here to feed an army. Some of the dishes sounded familiar but most were quite foreign to me." She laughed at her own joke. "Anyway, I figured we'd be able to find something to like. Honestly, I was feeling adventurous and wanted to try new French foods. Are you game?"

"Sure," Noah said, but he made no movement toward the food.

"Noah? Are you okay?"

"Yes. I'm great actually. I finished reading about you and Dad … and me. But I do have a question for you."

"Shoot."

"Why don't you publish Dad's story? Even though he's dead, it would still be an interesting love story. I think people would read it. It might touch them."

"I don't know. You might be able to convince me, but I'd have to think about it."

"You could call it, *The Apple of My Eye.*"

"Hmm. Maybe I will."

"I like what you wrote, Mom."

She set the food down at their feet and took the seat beside him. "It came from the heart."

"It was the stories I've always heard but with a context and somehow more real. I knew all about the crime and Dad ultimately taking a bullet to save the old guy. What I didn't know was that you were the one to piece it together. That's cool, Mom." He grinned at Brea before growing serious again. "And I didn't know about your struggle to forgive him. Any lingering anger I had washed away as I read that. I think that's why you should publish it. Not everyone does that—forgives. It's easier to hold a grudge and blame other people for your problems. I'm glad you're not like that."

"Thanks."

"The whole thing was really nice. I've been sitting out here ever since." He tipped his head toward his notebook sitting at his feet. Brea hadn't noticed it before.

"Writing your thoughts?"

"More than that. I reread those last two poems I wrote. Then I wrote a new one. It's for both of us—you and me, but I kept the same title. All this seems like one journey—a journey out of the shadows. It's just taken several steps to get there. Do you want to hear it?"

"Yes, I would." Brea turned her full attention on Noah.

Shadows
Our past shines bright behind us, warm upon our backs
Light hitting us, casting a shadow out before us
Showing, illuminating, directing our futures

Urging us—you and me,
Forward
Into the shadow cast ahead
And beyond,
Beyond shadows,
Beyond plans and shapes and darkened outlines
Into the unknown

Step out and beyond the shadow,
The shadow that
Pushes
Supports
Encourages
Urges
Forward
Onward

Those warm shadows and familiar shapes
Say, "We love you!"
Face forward
Go and do

Our past shines bright behind us,
Urging us—you and me,
Step out and beyond the shadow,
Go and do!

In the silence that followed, he softly said, "What do you think, Mom?"

"You're not asking if I like the poem, are you?"

Noah shook his head.

"I can, if you can," Brea said.

"I think *we* can."

"I love you, Noah. You are truly the apple of my eye."

Noah smiled and grabbed both of her hands in his. "Mom, you can have more than one happily ever after." He paused to let it sink in. "And yes, I wrote that saying in my notebook. But, seriously, Mom, I know you loved Dad, but you can love again. I'm not talking about having another man in your life. That doesn't matter either way. You can love your life and yourself. You can have a life. You can be Brea."

So soft Noah almost couldn't hear it, Brea said, "Yes, I can. For the first time in a dozen years, I believe I can." She turned to Noah with glistening eyes. "Would you just stop making me cry?"

Noah chuckled. "Not yet. I opened the next envelope. It said: *Do something your mom wants to do that you don't.*"

"Really? What could that be? Eating escargot?"

Noah smiled and stood up. Still holding her hands, he lifted her up from her chair. Then he wrapped his arms around her in a huge embrace— something he hadn't done in a very long time. Brea didn't even try to hold back the tears.

ENVELOPE #8

Brea enjoyed each of the dishes she had chosen, but that could have been a carryover from the surprising hug from her son, every worry and concern melting away in its aftermath. She didn't even try to suppress her smile.

Gathering the leftovers, she took in Noah's face. He was staring out at the Paris skyline, but his eyes weren't focused on anything in particular. He seemed to be far away with a contented visage she hadn't noticed for a long time. "What's on your mind, Noah?"

He turned at the sound of her voice. He shrugged but his smile didn't fade. "It wasn't bad."

"Which dish?"

"Not the food, although it was delicious. The hug, Mom. I could get used to that, maybe make a habit of it."

"I wouldn't mind that. And I promise not to tell your friends—the new ones I know you'll make."

"Deal."

. . .

After a good night's sleep, they spent the day sight-seeing, checking several of the famous Paris landmarks off their list. Returning to their room, they sorted through the books and souvenirs they'd purchased. "This better be our last stop or we'll never get everything home."

"We could mail it home," Noah suggested.

"Oh, you're right. Okay, then where next?"

Noah laughed. "I don't know. After Paris, probably home. Right now, are you up for going to the pool?"

"You have enough energy for swimming?"

"Yeah. Don't you?"

"Oh, you're being kind. But I wouldn't mind sitting poolside."

"Let's go then!"

"Now? What's your hurry?"

His face flushed. "When I filled up our ice bucket, I may have met a girl."

Brea sat up suddenly. "Oh?

"Don't get weird on me, Mom. She was cute and nice. She's headed to the pool and invited me to come. If you go with me, can you pretend not to know me?"

"That I can do. I promise."

. . .

François Couture was from the south of France. He and his daughter, Katriane, had come to spend the week in Paris. With an English word here and a French phrase from the internet there, Brea and François managed to have a pleasant conversation while their children chatted in the pool.

François' hair was a distinguished salt and pepper. His eyes lit up and his dimples flashed when he smiled. His voice was deep and clear. They visited in their halting manner for half an hour before Brea even thought of any comparisons with Paul. She smiled involuntarily at the thought.

"Okay? Something funny?" François asked, confusion etched on his face.

She wasn't sure how to explain to this man who would briefly float in and out her life that he'd made a difference. She had let him in. In the smallest degree, she'd let him in. And that was a huge step forward. "It's nothing. Umm, nil, zero …" She shrugged.

"Ah, *zéro*. Okay." But he still didn't understand the mysterious Mona Lisa smile on her lips.

. . .

"That was nice, Noah. I could get used to this new life."

"Do you like Katriane's dad?"

Brea shrugged. "I don't know. But I like being free to like him if I want. Or not. Life stretches before each of us as a blank slate. That's scary but mostly exciting." She reached out to Noah and he came near so she could put her arm around him. "Thank you."

"I've been thinking, Mom, about the power of words. What you wrote has made all the difference. And that got me thinking about the sayings in my notebook. I like all those things. But there's one phrase that keeps bothering me—'the apple doesn't fall far from the tree.' I know you were worried about me because I was hiding things and Dad hid things. So, that phrase … you only mentioned it once, but it's been like a dagger to me. It was all about the mistakes Dad made.

"When I read what you wrote about him, it reminded me that the conclusion you came to then and the one we've come to now is that he was a fallible person who was making good. We don't need to whitewash him, but his legacy is not about being perfect, it's about becoming—becoming better, working on improving and fixing things along the way. So, if that's how we feel about him, if we've really forgiven him for his mistakes, shouldn't we be focused on that?"

"Yes, we should. 'The apple doesn't fall far from the tree' can mean that. It doesn't have to be a negative phrase."

"I know, but I want a fresh start. You know how I told you I changed up that phrase about it's easier to get forgiveness than permission?"

"Didn't you change it to something like, 'It's easier not to be stupid in the first place'?"

"Yeah, something like that. So, I was thinking about a new phrase about being Dad's son. How about, 'A good tree brings forth good fruit'?"

"I like that, but I don't think it's original. I'm pretty sure that comes from the Bible."

"Yeah, I know. I told you I was collecting sayings and even making some up. This is one I'm collecting. I think it's useful for us."

Brea grinned. "You're right. It is. You are good fruit from a good tree."

"You're part of that tree, Mom." Noah wrapped her in a large embrace.

Brea hugged him back, reaching up with one hand to ruffle his hair. "Noah, you are definitely the apple of my eye."

. . .

Brea and Noah had agreed to meet François and Katriane for breakfast the next morning. Over their meal they made plans to spend the day together, taking in various sights the four of them had yet to see. It promised to be a great day.

But that wasn't the only reason.

Next to Martha's box in their hotel room, lay the last envelope, addressed to both Brea and Noah. The note was simple. When they opened it together, it made them smile.

> *Enjoy life even if you're not perfect at it. I think you can take it from here. (Don't make me come down there!)*
> *Love always,*
> *Martha/Mimi*

Perched next to the note was Brea's phone showing an image sent from her mother. Brea and Noah's apple tree filled the screen, the scars of recent damage overshadowed by hundreds of white-pink blossoms blanketing every limb.

ACKNOWLEDGMENTS

The creation of any book is a journey. Although I'd had requests for a sequel to *The Apple of My Eye*, I was content with where that story concluded. However, when Reagan Rothe of Black Rose Writing asked me to consider writing a sequel, I reevaluated my position. It took some time, but as I talked it over with my daughter, Amy, a natural story began to take shape. For whatever reason, I did not want to write a sequel where the woman who lost her husband in the first book finds true love again in the next. And so, it began to emerge as the story of a mother and son's relationship. A vehicle to explore that relationship took shape in the connections we have with our forebears. Having deeply forged bonds with ancestors myself, I have sprinkled variations of their names throughout this book from both my ancestral line and my husband's. I am grateful to them and the choices they made, making my life better and even possible.

Bringing this to fruition happened because of the help and support of many people. Nancy, with Row Venice (rowvenice.org) patiently and kindly answered all my questions. I hope to meet her in person soon. Jessica Scott Romano, a fellow author who now lives in Italy, provided excellent advice. I recommend her book *How to Be an American in Italy*. Any errors that remain are mine.

As always, I am grateful to the whole Black Rose Writing team, my fellow authors (who have become dear friends), and my family—particularly Amy, Steven, and my husband, Allen.

ABOUT THE AUTHOR

Mary Ellen Bramwell, an award-winning and best-selling author, has been writing short stories since she was ten. She is the mother of five and currently lives with her youngest son and her husband of over 35 years in the Mountain West. She enjoys reading, jigsaw puzzles, and playing games but is passionate about her family and alleviating the suffering of others.

NOTE FROM THE AUTHOR

Word-of-mouth is crucial for any author to succeed. If you enjoyed *The Apple Doesn't Fall Far*, please leave a review online—anywhere you are able. Even if it's just a sentence or two. It would make all the difference and would be very much appreciated.

Thanks!
Mary Ellen Bramwell

We hope you enjoyed reading this title from:

www.blackrosewriting.com

Subscribe to our mailing list – *The Rosevine* – and receive **FREE** books, daily
deals, and stay current with news about upcoming releases
and our hottest authors.
Scan the QR code below to sign up.

Already a subscriber? Please accept a sincere thank you for being a fan of
Black Rose Writing authors.

View other Black Rose Writing titles at
www.blackrosewriting.com/books and use promo code
PRINT to receive a **20% discount** when purchasing.

www.ingramcontent.com/pod-product-compliance
Lightning Source LLC
Chambersburg PA
CBHW070536100726
47907CB00004B/1138